SACRAMENTO PUBLIC LIBRARY

3 3029 05803 8700

SA ... ARY

D0350724

/2006

WITHDRAWN FROM COLLECTION
OF SACRAMENTO PUBLIC LIBRARY

The Bicycle Man

David L. Dudley

Clarion Books

New York

Clarion Books
a Houghton Mifflin Company imprint
215 Park Avenue South, New York, NY 10003
Copyright © 2005 by David L. Dudley

The text was set in 11-point Matt Antique.

All rights reserved.

For information about permission to reproduce selections from this
book, write to Permissions, Houghton Mifflin Company,
215 Park Avenue South, New York, NY 10003.

www.houghtonmifflinbooks.com

Printed in the U.S.A.

Library of Congress Cataloging-in-Publication Data

Dudley, David L.
The bicycle man / by David L. Dudley.
p. cm.
Summary: In poor, rural Georgia in 1927, twelve-year-old Carissa and
her suspicious mama take in an elderly drifter with a shiny bicycle, never
expecting how profoundly his wise and patient ways
will affect them.
ISBN 0-618-54233-7
[1. Country life—Georgia—Fiction. 2. African Americans—Fiction.
3. Single-parent families—Fiction. 4. Georgia—History—20th century—
Fiction.] I. Title.
PZ7.D86826Bic 2005
[Fic]—dc22
2005006409

ISBN-13: 978-0-618-54233-8
ISBN-10: 0-618-54233-7

MP 10 9 8 7 6 5 4 3 2 1

For Eileen,
who always believed

ONE

Summit, Georgia, 1927

I might never have met Bailey if Poppy hadn't decided to climb the magnolia tree. She had insisted we have a tea party with my doll, Zillah, in the cave formed by its low branches, which came all the way to the ground. Back when I was ten, the cave was my favorite secret place, and Zillah and I had played pretend there a lot. Now Zillah spent her time sitting on a shelf by my bed, except when Poppy came over. Poppy didn't have a doll of her own, even though she always bragged on how her mama gave her everything she asked for. I tried to tell her that tea parties didn't interest me anymore, now that I was twelve. She got that half-hurt, half-mad look that spelled trouble, so I gave in, as long as we could look at a book and not just talk baby talk to Zillah. Poppy agreed, so there we were, sitting in the shade under the tree, having our party.

"Drink your tea," I told her. "It's good."

Poppy sipped from her mug and made a face. "It ain't sweet," she complained. "I want sugar in mine."

"Mama said we can't have any sugar. Besides, it doesn't need any. Doesn't it make your mouth feel cool?" I had made the tea by crushing some mint leaves in a bowl and stirring them up with well water.

"It's nasty," Poppy said. "Ain't even hot."

"Zillah likes it." I held my mug to her mouth. "Don't you, Zillah?" I felt stupid offering a drink to a cloth doll, and annoyed with Poppy for being ungrateful.

Mama had made Zillah for my sixth birthday. She had been beautiful once, but her face and arms, made of brown cloth the same color as my skin, were faded and stained now. Her black yarn hair, braided into two pigtails, just like mine, was all frizzy because the yarn had frayed. I guess Zillah didn't know how shabby she looked. Her pink embroidered mouth remained frozen in its happy little smile.

"I don't want no more tea," Poppy declared, putting down her mug on the bare ground.

"Then I'll read to you."

"The one about the boat."

"That's the one you made me bring."

Poppy smiled, showing the gap where she'd lost both her front teeth. Mama asked her once if she'd knocked them out by running and falling, or by walking on a fence and crashing face-first onto the ground. Poppy said no, they'd come out on their own, with just a couple of yanks. Mama shook her head and told Poppy she was a mess. That's what Mama always said: "That girl is a mess, and her mama is sorry."

Looking at Poppy now, I had to agree. Her hair looked like nobody had tried to wash or comb it in days. It was brown with dust, and there were bits of leaves and grass in it. At the moment, her knees and elbows were crusted with dried mud, and the spaces between her toes were dark with dirt—leftovers from yesterday, when we'd played in mud puddles. Her dress needed washing, and so did her face. But Poppy didn't care, and neither did her mama.

"Read," she said.

The book was titled *My Adventures on the Seven Seas,* by Howard W. Armstrong. It had pictures, showing places he had visited all around the world, places with exotic names like Bora-Bora and Madagascar and the Cape of Good Hope. Mr. Armstrong's ship, a schooner with tall, straight masts and white sails that puffed in the wind, was named the *Pegasus.* But even more than the *Pegasus* and the different lands, I loved the pictures of the ocean. Poppy did, too. We had never been to an ocean or seen what Mr. Armstrong called "the majestic combers cresting and dashing downward during a squall at sea, only to rise yet again and hurl themselves forward, as if at the command of Old Neptune himself." That sentence had sent me to the dictionary at school to look up several words. My teacher, Miss Johnson, remarked that the author could have used simpler ones just as well. But I liked the sound of the fancy ones he had chosen.

"Chapter Four, 'Storm at Sea,'" I began.

Just then there was a crash from inside our cabin. It was Mama, knocking pots and pans together on the cook stove. She had been angry all day. The dog next door had killed one of our chickens, and now we were down to three. There had been ugly words between Mama and Mrs. Washington, the hound's owner. Mrs. Washington had offered to buy Mama another pullet when she got the money together, but Mama had yelled that Mrs. Washington wasn't going to *ever* get the money together because no one had any money. When it was over, Mrs. Washington had gone off saying how stuck up Mama was and how she should understand that sometimes dogs just get full of themselves and do that kind of thing. Mama had stalked into our cabin, complaining about how much she hated Summit and the South and wishing we were back north, where we belonged.

"Your mama still some mad," Poppy declared.

"I know. Hush now, and let me read." The *Pegasus* had gotten caught in a hurricane in the Atlantic Ocean.

"Show the pictures."

"When I come to them," I said. "Can't you wait?"

The minute I started reading again, Poppy jumped up and headed for the trunk of the tree. She grabbed a branch, pulled herself up, and started to climb.

"I won't read if you're going to play."

No reply. Poppy reached for the next higher branch and scrambled up.

"You'll fall," I told her.

She just kept going.

I closed my book, put it on the piece of cloth I'd brought to keep it from getting dirty, and stood up. "Come down right now!" I shouted. "That's dangerous."

"It fun! C'mon."

"I can't. Mama says if I climb a tree, I'll fall and break my neck. Come down!"

Branches high up in the tree rattled.

"I'll tell Mama, and you'll get in trouble."

Poppy only laughed. Now she had disappeared completely, hidden by a mass of glossy dark green leaves.

I crawled out from our cave and went into the road, where the red clay was warm under my bare feet. I craned my neck upward, trying to spot Poppy.

"Carissa!" she called.

"Where are you?"

"Up here. See me?"

"No. Where?"

"I's looking right at you."

Now I spotted her face, half-hidden among the leaves. Then she poked out a skinny arm and started waving at me.

"Don't do that!" I cried. "Hold on! You'll fall and kill yourself."

"I can see Fifteen-Mile Creek."

"No, you can't. It's too far away."

"Can, too. Up here you can see the whole world. I sees Swainsboro over yonder."

"You're lying!" I shouted. "That's eleven miles! Deacon Braithwaite says so!"

"How he know? He ain't never been up this high. Ohh! There's Atlanta, way yonder."

My patience was gone. "I'm telling Mama!"

"'Afternoon," said a voice just behind my left shoulder.

I jumped because I hadn't heard anyone coming. Beside me was an old man—older even than Granma. He wore a crumpled hat and was clenching a battered pipe in his teeth. He needed a shave—silver bristles covered the deep brown skin of his cheeks and chin—but his eyes were gentle. With his faded shirt, baggy pants, and patched jacket, the man looked like a tramp. He carried a pack on his back— a bedroll.

We had been seeing a lot of tramps. Mama said times were hard and some people were poor, even poorer than we were. But this man was different. He was standing in the dirt road holding the handlebars of the newest, shiniest blue bicycle I had ever seen.

"Hey!" Poppy called from her perch high above us. She waved.

"She won't come down," I told the man. "She's going to fall and break every bone in her body."

"That so?" the man said. He didn't say it like he was worried.

"She always runs and climbs and does what she shouldn't. That's why she always has cuts and bruises. Mama says one day she's going to kill herself. Maybe today is the day."

"I doubt it," the man said. "Folks spry enough to git up so high can usually figure a way to git back down without bustin' anything. . . . Air nice up there?" he called to Poppy.

"I can see Atlanta!" she crowed.

"Quit lying," I demanded. "Come down right now."

"Get away from her, you old tramp!" shrilled a voice from our front porch. Mama came striding toward us, wiping her hands on a feed-sack towel. "Go on! You've got no business bothering a child."

"'Afternoon, missuz," the man answered pleasantly. "Mighty hot for September, ain't it?"

"Look there." I pointed to the top of the magnolia.

"Hey, there, Miz Lorena," Poppy called.

Mama clapped her hand over her mouth. "O my sweet Lord Jesus. That girl's final day has arrived at last. You, Poppy!" she shouted. "Quit playing the fool and get down here this minute!"

"Shh," the man told Mama. "No need for that. If we stay nice and calm, she'll come down."

"I don't know you," Mama shot back at him. "Who are you to be telling me my business?"

"I ain't tryin' to do that. But it seems to me that young'un is havin' herself a high ol' time, bein' the center of all our attention. If we let her be, she'll come down soon enough."

"And what if she falls?"

"She ain't gon' fall. Besides, what can we do about it if she does? There ain't no way *I* can climb up and help her down. No, ma'am. She'll find her own way, jus' like she did goin' up."

Mama looked him up one side and down the other, like she was trying to decide whether to listen to him or not.

"Let's go over into the shade," the man suggested. "Take away her audience." He started wheeling his bicycle toward the magnolia tree.

I was surprised when Mama followed him. "Come on," she told me. When we were in the shade, Mama faced the man. "Where'd you get that bicycle?" she asked suspiciously. "Stole it, I reckon."

Was Mama right? I'd been too interested in the bicycle itself to wonder how the man had gotten it. He didn't look like he had enough money to buy his supper, let alone pay for a fancy bike.

"No, ma'am. It's mine. Bought from Sears, Roebuck and Company in Chicago."

"How'd you get to Chicago? That's hundreds of miles away."

"I ain't been there myself, but a man can order from a catalog."

"Where'd you get the money for a bike like that? No colored folks I know have that kind of money."

I couldn't tell why Mama was asking so many questions. But now I wanted to hear the man's story, too.

"Hey," Poppy called from her lookout.

"Don't answer her," the man said. "I earned the money myself, missuz."

"How?"

"Doin' odd jobs here and there." He pulled out a frayed handkerchief and wiped his forehead. "Might I trouble you folks for a drink o' water? It sho' is hot today, and I've been on the road since dawn."

Mama looked him over *again,* and then studied the bicycle. So did I. No colored child I knew had a bicycle, and the bikes owned by the white children in town were dented and scratched from rough use. But this one gleamed as if it had come straight off the train from Chicago not fifteen minutes ago. I didn't know how to ride a bicycle because no one had ever offered me a chance to learn. Besides, if I did try, I'd surely fall off and hurt myself. Maybe break my arm. Still, I wanted to touch it, feel the smooth metal under my fingers.

"You weren't messing with my daughter?" Mama asked.

"No, ma'am. I was comin' along, and I saw her in the road, talkin' to that magnolia tree. 'What's goin' on?' I asked myself. 'Must be somethin' strange. Little girls don't usually talk to trees.'"

"Where y'all go?" Poppy shouted from above.

The man put his finger to his lips.

Then Mama made her decision. "Carissa, go get the man a dipper of water."

"What a pretty name," he said.

That stopped me in my tracks. Nobody in Summit had ever said a thing about my name except to tell Mama—right in front of me—what an odd name I had. They told her nobody *they* knew had such a strange name, and they wondered what Mama was thinking when she branded me with a name that folks would talk about my whole life. Then they wanted to know how old I was, and when Mama told them, the next thing they'd say was, "Isn't she mighty small for her age?"

"Where'd you get such a pretty name?" he asked me.

"Mama picked it."

"It means 'dearest,'" Mama noted with pride. "From a Latin word. *Carissima*. I read it in a book once and thought it sounded real pretty."

"Sho' 'nough?" The man thought a moment. "'Dearest.' Fits, don't it?"

Mama eyed me skeptically. "It fits most of the time." Then she recollected herself. "Why are you standing there like a statue? Didn't I tell you to get the man some water?"

I scampered round back. When I returned, walking

slowly so as not to spill it, he took the dipper and drank it dry in one gulp.

"Do you need more?" Mama asked.

"If it ain't too much trouble." So I was sent again. When I came back this time, there was Poppy, standing with her back to Mama, who had hold of her dress so tight that she couldn't move.

I gave the man the dipper; he drank again and said he was satisfied. Then he looked at Poppy. "Welcome back to earth," he said. "Glad to make yo' acquaintance."

Poppy held both hands to her face and giggled like she was all embarrassed to meet a stranger.

"You just about gave me a heart attack," Mama declared. She turned Poppy around and glared at her. "If I *ever* catch you in that tree again, I'm going to wear you out, even if you aren't my own child. I reckon someone has to try to pound some sense into you. Do you understand?"

Poppy nodded.

"You say 'Yes, ma'am' when I speak to you!"

"Yes, ma'am," she whispered.

"Now go home. I've had enough of your mess for one afternoon. And don't ask if Carissa can come down later on, because she can't. Or tomorrow, either. It's a big wash day and I'll need her all day. Now get going!"

Poppy backed toward the road, and as she passed the blue bicycle, she ran her hand over the fender.

"Who said you could touch that?" Mama cried. "Go!"

Poppy grinned at me and took off down the road.

Mama looked after her, shaking her head. "What a mess." She turned to the man. "I appreciate your advice," she said. "You were right."

The man didn't say anything, as if he was waiting for Mama to continue. She didn't, though. The three of us just stood silent under the magnolia tree. "Well, I'd better be gettin' on," he said at last. "Thank you for the water. Nice to meet you, Carissa." He wheeled his bicycle to the road, swung his leg over, and began to push off.

"Wait," Mama said. "I reckon you're hungry."

He stopped. "Reckon I am."

"What'd you think you were going to do for supper?"

"I got some pork and beans in my pack. Thought I'd open 'em when I get down the road some and stop for the night."

"I can fix you a plate," Mama told him.

"I'd be much obliged."

"I'll bring something out. Carissa, come help."

I followed Mama inside. As I went through the door, I saw the man still standing over the bicycle. He winked at me.

Mama cut some corn bread and put a pot of beans on the cook stove to heat. It was plenty hot in the house. We had two rooms, the bigger one for cooking and sitting. A door in the far wall opened to our back yard. To the right of this room was another, smaller one, where Mama and I shared a rickety old iron bed and hung our clothes on pegs hammered into the wall. The cook stove made the kitchen room so hot in summer that I couldn't stand it, but Mama said that being uncomfortable was part of life, like disappointment and unhappiness. You just had to accept the heat because there was not one thing you could do about it.

"Get a plate, a spoon, and a cup," Mama directed me. She poured some syrup on the corn bread and dished up some beans. "Get some water and tell him to come to the porch."

I filled the mug with water from the bucket and carried it out to the front porch. The man had brought the bicycle into the yard and was standing in the shade, fanning himself with his hat.

"Mama says come on the porch," I told him.

He did. Mama came out of the door with the plate of food. "Here," she offered.

He took the plate. "Thank you, missuz. Much obliged. Mind if I sit down?"

"Help yourself," Mama told him, nodding at a weather-beaten rocking chair. "Come on, Carissa."

Once we were back inside, I asked Mama, "Why didn't you invite him in?"

"I can't have a strange man in the house. What'd folks say? We don't know a thing about him. I shouldn't even have given him supper. Don't know why I did. Lord knows we can't spare it." Mama went to the stove and began dishing beans onto a plate.

"Are we going to eat now?" I asked. "It's too early."

"Now, if you want your supper warm. I'm not going to fire up this stove another time today. It's too hot."

Cold beans didn't sound good, so I let Mama go ahead.

While we were eating, there was a knock on the door, and Mama got up to answer it. I started to get up, too, but she motioned to me to stay put.

When Mama opened the door, I could see the man on the porch. She went out, pulling the door partway closed behind her. The man said something and Mama answered, but I couldn't hear what they were saying.

Mama came back inside, holding the mug and empty plate. She turned and looked out the door for a minute, as if waiting for something to happen. Then she came to the table. "He's gone. I still think he stole that bicycle. A man that age on something like that sure does look ridiculous."

I wished Mama had let me say goodbye. And that I'd seen him riding his bike, too. But by the time I finished my corn bread and helped Mama wash up, I knew it was too late. He was long gone.

Two

That night, I dreamed about the Bicycle Man. He was riding his blue bicycle through the streets of Chicago. Of course, I had no idea what Chicago actually looked like because I hadn't been there—or anywhere else that I could recall. Summit was all I knew, except for Swainsboro, where we went once in a while on shopping days.

I had been born in the North, in Philadelphia, where Daddy had gone to find work and where he met Mama. She had been raised in an orphanage run by white people and was working in a store when she met Daddy. They got married and had me, but when I was only two, Daddy enlisted and got killed in France. "Your daddy was a hero," Mama always told me. She said I must never forget he died fighting for his country and that I should be proud of him.

After Daddy was killed, Mama was in bad trouble. She had no money and no job, so she wrote to Daddy's mother in Georgia, asking for help. Granma wrote back, inviting Mama and me to come stay with her for a while. Mama accepted, and Summit had been our home for ten years.

I lay beside Mama, dreaming that the Bicycle Man and I were parading down a Chicago street while people stared at that handsome bicycle and asked whose it was. And he would say, "It belongs to this dear little girl. Want to see her ride it?" I would climb on, and he would push me. Off I would go, flying down those crowded streets.

A sound woke me up. It was after dawn—the faint light coming through the window told me that, as did the crowing of a rooster off somewhere. I knew the sound: the chopping of wood. It was so close that it seemed to be in our own back yard.

I slipped out of bed, smoothed my nightdress down over my legs, tiptoed to the back door, and peeked out. There was the Bicycle Man at the woodpile, chopping away and singing to himself while he worked. He had already made a good-size stack of split logs. The bicycle leaned against the catalpa tree.

"Mama," I said, hurrying back to the bedroom. "Mama, wake up."

"What is it?" she asked groggily.

"The Bicycle Man."

"Who?" She sat up and I knew she heard the sound now, too.

"The Bicycle Man. He's chopping wood for us."

"What?" Mama jumped out of bed, pulled on her robe, and went barefooted to the door. I followed her.

"What do you think you're doing?" she called out.

"'Mornin'," he said, tipping his hat. He'd taken off his jacket, and there were dark patches under his arms where his shirt was wet.

"I asked what you are doing," Mama repeated slowly. "There's no place for a man here. I can't afford to feed you, and I can chop wood myself."

"Missuz, I had to repay you for my supper."

"I thought you were long gone," Mama shot back. "When you rode off last night, you should have kept going."

"That was my plan, missuz. Then when I made camp, I said to myself, 'Bailey, you can't jus' eat a poor woman's food and not repay her. That ain't the way you was taught.'"

Bailey. The Bicycle Man had a name! I liked it. Mr. Bailey. Or maybe Bailey was his first name.

"I don't care how you were taught," Mama said. "Nobody asked you to chop our wood. Now, please go. There's no place around here for you."

"Today's wash day, ain't it?"

"How do you know that?" Mama sounded suspicious.

"You said so yourself, yesterday evenin'."

"What does wash day have to do with anything?"

"If you're gon' wash, you got to have wood for the fire. So here's some wood. But you're gon' need more, I'll bet. As much wash as you do."

"How do you know how much wash I do?" Mama tied her robe, stepped outside, went down the steps, and planted herself in the hard red clay at the bottom.

"You wash for the white folks, don't you?"

"Who told you that? Have you been sticking your nose into my business, talking to folks about me?"

Mama's voice was rising, the way it did when she was ready to fight. But Mr. Bailey hadn't done anything wrong, as far as I could tell. I hoped there wasn't going to be a shouting match. Scenes like that scared me. Mr. Bailey didn't seem like a man who would yell at a woman, though. He was too polite.

"Missuz," he said, "I ain't asked no one about you. But I got to figurin'. I ain't seen no man round the place, and a colored woman alone with a child got to have *some* way of makin' a living. Round here, she got two choices: cook for the white folks or wash for 'em. Maybe both. You do wash. Lots of it, I bet."

"What if I do? I can manage my work myself. Now, put down my ax and please go away."

Just then there was a knock at the front door. "That's your granma," Mama told me. "Go let her in and tell her to come right here."

Granma stood on the porch, panting, the sweat running down her face, making little channels through the coating of fine dust on her cheeks. Reaching for a bandana tucked in her apron pocket, she mopped her face. "It's right hot already," she gasped. "Bendin' over dat boilin' pot all day is gon' be like sufferin' de torments o' hell." Bailey was right: Mama and Granma did wash for several white ladies, and Monday was their day for doing sheets and towels.

Granma was dressed as she was every day except Sunday, in a long-sleeved cotton blouse that buttoned up the front, a skirt that hung to her ankles, and heavy work shoes that once had been brown but now were stained the same orange-red as the clay road. A blue gingham apron with enormous pockets was tied about her waist.

"Mama says go to her," I reported.

"*Says?* Since when do Lorena order me to do somethin'?"

"I mean, she *asks* if you could please go to her."

"Where she at?"

I nodded, and followed Granma across the room to the back door.

"What is it, Lorena?" she asked.

"I made the mistake of feeding an old tramp last night, and now he's here chopping wood and won't go away. I told him to leave, but he won't."

Bailey tipped his hat but said nothing.

"Lorena, come up here," Granma commanded. "I needs to talk to yuh."

When Mama got to the top of the steps, Granma yanked her into the room. "'Mornin'," she called out to Bailey. "Wait dere a minute." Then she pulled the back door closed. "Yuh wants to run him off?" she asked Mama, as if it was the craziest notion she'd ever heard.

"Of course I do! I can't have a man around here."

"At least let him chop all de wood he want. An' what's so bad about a man roun' de place?"

"Miz Rachel, what are you talking about? He's a stranger. I've got no work for him to do, and I can't feed him. Besides, it's not right for a widow to have a man around."

"He too old fer yuh anyhow."

"Then you take him," Mama retorted.

I was used to hearing Mama and Granma go back and forth like this, but they never really got mad and stayed mad.

Granma chuckled. "Mens is hard to come by, Lorena. Young mens all gone north or married to no-account local gals. Ol' men all dead or crippled or crazy in dey minds. An' yuh's gon' turn away a able-bodied man who wants t' chop wood without bein' *asked?*"

Mama looked disgusted. Granma opened the door. "You dere," she called. "You finish choppin' wood fer us, we fix yuh some breakfast."

Soon it was time to do the washing. In the yard, Bailey already had a fire going under the wash pot, which he had filled with water from the well. "Thought you ladies could use some help," he said.

"We can manage on our own," Mama declared. Granma poked her in the back.

Bailey seemed not to notice. "By the way, missuz, that was a mighty fine breakfast you cooked."

"There's nothing special about grits and biscuits with syrup."

"Excuse me, missuz, but could I know your name?"

"I don't see why. You'll be gone from here in a few minutes, now you've been fed."

"Her name Lorena Hudson," Granma broke in. "And I's Miz Rachel Hudson."

"Please to meet you both," Bailey said. "And of course I already know Carissa."

"What yo' name?" Granma asked.

"Bailey," Mama told her.

"Jus' Bailey?"

"That's all," he answered.

"Dat yo' first name or yo' last name?"

"First. Had a last name once, but it came from the whites that owned my daddy, so when I left home, I dropped it and decided to go by plain Bailey. It's always been enough."

"You can't order anything from a Sears, Roebuck catalog with just a first name," Mama said triumphantly.

"You can if the postmaster knows you. He wrote 'Mr. B. Bailey' for me. Bailey Bailey. Guess that's my full name."

"We thanks yuh for yo' help, Mr. Bailey," Granma said.

"You welcome, Miz Rachel."

"And now you can be on your way," Mama added. Granma poked her again. "Quit it, Miz Rachel. It *is* time for him to go."

"Mr. Bailey, I 'pologize fer mah daughter-in-law's bad manners," Granma said. "She don't mean nothin' by it. We ain't got much, but what we got, yuh's welcome to a bit of, long as yuh kin work fer it."

Mama turned away.

"I appreciate that, Miz Rachel," Bailey answered. "I see y'all ain't got much. Who has? And I couldn't take nothin' for free. But I kinda like it round here, and the place *could* use some work."

Bailey was right about that. The fence needed fixing, the henhouse wall had a hole big enough to let in a hungry dog, and our roof leaked in the bedroom. Mr. Thompson, who owned our cabin, was supposed to fix all that. Mama kept on asking him, and he kept on saying he would, but he never did. Mama said he was "sorry." She said she hoped and prayed that one day we could go back north, where colored folks could live decent lives.

Sometimes at night, Mama and I would lie in bed and talk. "We won't always live here," she told me more than once.

"Where will we go? Philadelphia? Is that a good place?"

"Better than this."

"Are people nice there? Would I have friends?"

"Of course you would, sugar. And up there, you don't have to know everyone and everyone doesn't know you. There are *way* too many folks for that to be possible. So you can choose your friends, and nobody else has to know your business."

"When can we go?" I'd ask.

"Soon," she would always tell me.

But "soon" never arrived. . . .

Bailey was standing there, ax in hand, ready to help, but Mama wanted to be rid of him. I didn't understand it.

"We can make it on our own," she told him again. "So thank you, and now you can be moving on."

"Lorena, I needs to speak to yuh," Granma said. "'Scuse us, Mr. Bailey."

When she had tugged Mama back into the house, Granma said firmly, "Lorena, don't be a fool. De man is offerin' to stay around fer a while an' help us, but yuh's tryin' yo' hardes' to scare him off."

I was happy to hear Granma say that. Doing the laundry was backbreaking work. We had to build the fire, bring water from the well, and fill the pot, then let the clothes boil before we scrubbed them. Then we had to rinse them in cool water, wring them as dry as we could, and hang them on the line. After that came the starching and ironing. Granma was right. Mama should be glad for any help anyone wanted to give.

But there was more to it than that. Bailey was something new. Most of the time, my life was dull, what with the same few people to talk to, the same few places to visit, and the same endless chores to do. Bailey might make the world more exciting. Besides, he seemed to be a kind man. I couldn't say why, exactly, but I liked him a lot.

"Miz Rachel, how can I feed him?" Mama asked. "A man needs plenty of food. And where is he going to sleep?"

"He kin sleep in de shed. Put a pallet in dere, clean it up some, an' it be fine fer him."

Mama looked at Granma hard. "Maybe he *could* stay at your place," she suggested. "Maybe you've just found that husband you've been looking for all these years."

"Maybe," Granma replied calmly. "I jus' knows I ain't gon' turn down a blessing jus' 'cause o' mah pride."

"What's wrong with pride?"

"Nothin', 'cept when it's too expensive."

"What do you mean?"

"Lorena, pride is like dat red hat in Hall's store I been wantin'. I love dat hat an' sho' would like to have it, but it cost too much. No matter how much I wants it, it ain't fer me. Same's true 'bout pride an' every colored woman I knows. Pride be nice to have, but we can't afford it."

"It seems to *me* that pride is the one thing I shouldn't have to buy," Mama retorted. "It's the one thing I know I have, and no one is going to take it from me."

"That's a high-soundin' speech, but pride never chopped me no wood."

Mama set her jaw and didn't answer.

"Yuh keep yo' pride, honey," Granma said, patting Mama on the shoulder, "if it's dat important to yuh. But we gotta live in dis world, too. You need some help. So do I. Bailey say he like it here. It kin all work out. Let him stay. If yuh don't, I *am* gon' invite him down to mah place, an' den we'll see how folks talk."

"All right," Mama sighed. "But this is going to make trouble."

Beaming in victory, Granma opened the back door. I stood beside her, but Mama turned away and added some more wood to the cook stove.

"Mr. Bailey," Granma said, "mah daughter an' I agrees dat if yuh wants to stay here fer a few days, yuh's welcome. You kin sleep in dat shed dere, an' if yuh help us round dis place an' mah place down de road, we kin feed yuh some. But dat's all. We ain't got no money to pay yuh. Agreed?"

"Thank you, ma'am. I can earn my keep. I know how to do all kinds o' work, and the place does need some fixin' up."

"Yuh's right about dat. Summit is jus' down de road three miles, an' wid yo' bicycle, you could get dere in no time. Maybe you kin pick up some jobs right in town."

"I'll see 'bout it. Thank you for the advice."

"We can't stand here talking all morning," Mama broke in. "My laundry isn't getting done by itself. Carissa, bring those bags of sheets so we can get them into the boiling pot."

"Let me," Bailey offered from the yard.

He kept the fire going all morning, lifted steaming laundry from the water, and even helped hang sheets and towels on the line. When it was late afternoon, he insisted on pulling the wagon while Mama and Granma delivered towels in town. The sheets would have to wait until they had been ironed the next day, when we would also wash shirts, dresses, and underwear.

I didn't usually go to town, because I wasn't needed and it was six miles there and back, but that day I did, to see what people would do when they saw a strange man with us. The whites didn't even seem to notice Bailey standing silently in their yards while Mama and Granma delivered towels to back doors and took their money. It was the colored people who turned to look at us when they passed us on the road and came to front porches to stare and whisper as we went by. Mama said we'd make a week's worth of gossip.

As Mama and I got supper that evening, Bailey swept the shed in the yard. Then he went up to Granma's to bring back a pallet she wasn't using.

When supper was ready—beans, greens, a bit of fat meat, and bread—Mama had me take a plate out to where he sat on the back steps, smoking his pipe.

"My little place is gon' be right comfortable," he said, putting his pipe down and accepting the food. "I can build a frame for the pallet, to get it up off the floor, and make me a table and a stool. Soon as I earn some money, I'll buy a lantern. Maybe even try to find an old stove, jus' a small one for heat. Run a stovepipe through the back wall, if your mama'll let me."

"I'm glad you're staying," I told him.

"What a sweet thing to say! I 'preciate that."

"It was nice of you to help us today."

"Glad t' do it. Never hurts to lend a hand when you can. Kindness always has a way of comin' back to you, sooner or later."

"I like you," I said.

"But your mama ain't so sure about me."

I said nothing.

"It's all right. She's a cautious woman. Ain't nothin' wrong with that." He paused. "Where's your daddy?"

"Dead. He was killed in the war."

"I'm sorry."

"We're not from around here," I added. "Mama wants to go back to Philadelphia, but we don't have enough money."

"I see," he said, spooning up some beans. "Maybe we can help her."

"How?"

"Let me think about it."

"Carissa, get in here and eat your supper," Mama called from the door.

"I don't want you to get friendly with that man," she told me as I sat down to eat. "Stay clear of him. We don't know a thing about him, no matter what your granma says. The sooner he goes, the happier I'll be."

"He's nice," I said.

"And just how do you know that? A stranger gives us one day's work, and suddenly you've decided he's nice? You'll find out that folks can act nice one minute, then turn around and do you dirt the next."

"Why don't you trust him, Mama?"

She thought for a moment. "A lifetime of disappointments, that's why. And why are you so sure that he's nice? Tell me, because I'd really like to know."

Now it was my turn to stop and think, but I couldn't explain. "Just a feeling," I said at last.

"Hmmph," Mama said. "Feelings have cost a lot of people a lot of heartache, I can tell you. Better use your head and put your feelings on the shelf."

I wanted to answer, to defend Bailey and my own sureness that he was truly good and kind. But Mama was right. All I had to go on were my feelings and Bailey's one day of help. Maybe that wasn't enough.

THREE

The next morning, Bailey went up to Granma's to see what work needed to be done. Not five minutes later, our neighbor, Delia Washington, came to the door, a basket of scuppernong grapes in her hands.

"'Mornin', Lorena," she said.

"'Morning," Mama said.

"Feels like it gon' be another hot day."

"I reckon." Mama had planted herself in the doorway, arms folded.

"Look, Lorena, I's right sorry about what that no-account dog o' mine done to yo' hen. I knows yuh can't spare even one pullet. Nobody can. I done said I was gon' replace it when I gets the money, and I intends to keep mah promise. When pecans come in, I'll have me some extra money. So if yuh kin wait jus' a little while, I'll make good on it. In the meantime, I brought yuh some ripe scuppernongs. They's right good. I bet Carissa would enjoy 'em."

Mama accepted the grapes. "Thank you, Miz Washington."

"You jus' call me Delia. We's lived next door to one another so long, ain't no reason fer yuh to be so formal." Mrs. Washington peered past Mama, as if she was looking for something. Maybe she was hoping Mama would invite her to sit and have some coffee.

But Mama didn't. "That's kind of you, Miz Washington."

"Delia," Mrs. Washington reminded her.

"Delia. I wish I could ask you to sit awhile, but I have work to do. You know how it is."

Mrs. Washington looked disappointed. "'Course I do. I'll jus' go on and let y'all get on with yo' day." Mama took a step forward, as if to hurry her along, but Delia Washington wasn't quite ready to go. "By the way, I couldn't help notice that man yuh got round here. He must be some of yo' kin from up north. Yo' uncle, maybe?"

"No, *Miz Washington*. He's no relation. The man's just a traveler passing through. He was nice enough to offer to help out for a couple days in exchange for some home cooking. As you can see, he's sleeping in the shed, because I won't have a stranger in my house, even one who offers to do some chores for me."

As Mama spoke, her voice got louder and louder. The memory of her recent run-in with Mrs. Washington rose up in me. I hated it when Mama quarreled with someone, even when I knew she was right. When the fight was over, she had a way of staying angry, sometimes for days. Then she was hard to live with, even though she wasn't upset with me.

"One more thing," Mama said. "The man might be a stranger, but he's showed me more kindness than some of the people on this road. And you can tell that to any other snoops who are dying to find out my business. Now, if you will excuse me, I have work to do."

Mrs. Washington stood like a mule that's just been hit on the head with a two-by-four. Then she realized she'd been insulted. "Well!" she exclaimed. "I comes here tryin' to be neighborly, and this is what I git. For years I been sayin' that yuh ain't as high an' mighty as some say yuh is, but I guess I was wrong. And if yuh wants to finish ruinin' yo' reputation by lettin' some strange man live with yuh, then I reckon that's yo' business."

Mrs. Washington stomped down the porch steps, nearly running over Poppy, who was coming up. "Out o' mah way, girl," she growled. She stomped across the yard and pushed her way through the gate so fiercely that it pulled away from its one good hinge and fell into the dust.

"You can pay for my gate when you replace that hen!" Mama shouted. But Mrs. Washington just kept going.

Mama came back into the room, Poppy right behind her. She advanced toward the table and slammed down the basket with such force that several scuppernongs flew out and landed on the floor. "That woman doesn't care a thing about our dead hen or about being neighborly. It was all an excuse to get in here and learn about Bailey. Then she'd have something juicy to chew over when all the old cows get together for gossip. What a fool I am," she muttered. "Losing my temper and giving her even more to talk about. Carissa, get these grapes out of my sight. I'd choke on them if I tried to eat even one."

"Come on," I told Poppy, taking the basket.

We went to our place under the magnolia tree. The scuppernongs looked good—large and plump with golden brown skin. The first one I ate tasted even better than it looked. The juice just under the skin was like sugar syrup. I separated the skin from the flesh of the grape with my tongue and then spit out the skin. I ate the pulp slowly, catching the seeds between my lower teeth and gums, spitting them out when the rest of the grape was gone.

Poppy crammed a grape into her mouth, chewed, and swallowed it, skin and all. She ate three while I was working on one.

"Are you swallowing the seeds?" I asked.

She shook her head.

"What are you doing with them?"

By way of answer, Poppy spit one right at me, hitting me square on the forehead. She laughed.

"I'll get you back," I threatened. I put another grape into my mouth and bit into it. But when I tried to launch a seed through my puckered lips, it went about a foot and landed in the dirt. Poppy thought that was funny, too, so funny that she spit another seed at me. So I tried again and got her on the cheek. Soon we were gobbling grapes and waging seed war against each other, giggling like two fools.

When we'd worn out the game, I noticed that my dress front was covered with juice stains and bits of slimy pale yellow pulp. Mama was going to let me have it, for sure.

"My stomach hurts," Poppy complained.

"Serves you right. Look how many you ate. You gobbled just like a hog."

"So did you."

"I did not."

"Did so."

"Did not!" But my stomach didn't feel so good, either. I pushed the basket aside.

"Let's go down to my house," Poppy suggested. "Get Zillah and we'll play."

"I don't want to play with her."

"Then let me. I'll be careful."

"Let's just go."

"Please? Go inside and get her."

"Oh, all right."

"Your mama gon' be outdone when she see your dress."

I brushed the front of it, trying to get rid of the bits of pulp. "Is that better?"

"Nope."

"It's all your fault. You started it."

"It was fun."

"Your fun always makes trouble."

"Maybe *I* could get Zillah," Poppy volunteered. "I'll tell your mama you in the outhouse and ask if we can go to my place. Then my mama wash your dress and hang it out to dry. Your mama never even know."

I liked that idea. Mama was already upset about Mrs. Washington. If she saw my stained dress, she would really be angry.

"What would I wear while my dress was being washed and dried?"

"One o' my dresses. I got extra."

"Your dresses are too small for me. I'm four years older than you and a lot bigger."

"No, you ain't a lot bigger. Mama say you small for your age."

"I am not!"

Poppy was right, though. I was twelve, but I hadn't started showing any signs of what Granma called my "womanhood." I still looked like a stick, while some girls my own age were already growing hips and bosoms. At school, they were the ones the boys noticed, while I was ignored. It wasn't fair, and it didn't help when Mama told me that my time would come soon enough.

"Mama give you somethin' o' hers," Poppy said. "She got plenty."

"She's too big."

"Jus' wear your drawers, then. Ain't nobody gon' care."

"All right," I said.

"You go to the outhouse, and I'll ask if we can go."

"What if Mama says no?"

Poppy shrugged. "If we don't ask, we sure won't have no chance."

I went to the outhouse and closed the door behind me. Inside it was hot and still. A granddaddy longlegs crawled down the back wall to meet me. Mama always said you had to watch out for black widow spiders in an outhouse. For some reason, they loved to hide there and bite you when you were sitting down, defenseless.

Poppy knocked, and I came out to find her carelessly holding Zillah by the leg. Poppy didn't know how to take care of anything.

"Come on," she urged. "Let's go before your mama want to speak to you."

"It's all right?" I asked, rescuing Zillah.

"Yeah. She said you be home in time to help get supper. Now c'mon."

We sneaked from the outhouse and went through

the woods behind Mrs. Washington's place. When we were out of sight of our cabin, Poppy and I came back to the road.

"I hope my dress gets dry in time," I said as we walked toward the hollow where Poppy lived.

"If it don't, we'll say that we was at the creek and you fell in."

"It's not right to lie."

"Lyin' save you a heap o' trouble sometimes. And ain't we *already* tellin' your mama a lie?"

Poppy had a point, if not telling the whole truth was the same as a lie. Mama would have said so—that was certain.

The road sloped toward the creek bottom where Poppy and her mother lived. Some live oaks spread their branches overhead, creating shade and a little coolness. A deer fly kept buzzing around my face and trying to land on my head. Maybe he smelled the sticky juice down my front.

Poppy's house was a two-room cabin like ours, nestled under three live oaks. Miss Dolores, Poppy's mother, was sitting on the porch, rocking and cooling herself with a palmetto-leaf fan.

"Hey, sugar," Miss Dolores called to her daughter. "Hey, there, Miss Carissa. What you two been up to?"

Miss Dolores looked cool and comfortable, despite the heat. She was wearing a pink dress with a ruffle around the neckline and at the hem. Gold-colored hoop earrings hung from her pierced ears, and a pink bow was fastened in her curled hair. Miss Dolores smelled good, too, just like she always did. Once, she put some of her perfume on me, but Mama made me wash it off with soap when I got home.

Miss Dolores always looked good, but she didn't care a thing about how Poppy looked. Poppy could go for days without getting her hair washed and combed. Her dresses usually looked ten times as dirty as mine did now. Sometimes Miss Dolores would bathe Poppy every day and put powder and cologne on her, too. That never lasted very long, though, and soon Poppy would be back to her usual shabby-looking self. She said she liked it better that way. All those baths and combings made her tired.

Miss Dolores didn't do the same kind of work all the other women did. Mama, Delia Washington, Mama's friend Alma, and the ladies at Holy Zion Church all did washing, cleaning, and cooking for the white folks. Not Miss Dolores. She worked nights at Snoosy's Place, north on Canoochee Road. Mama said Snoosy's Place was nothing but a juke joint, where folks who weren't good, upstanding Christians went to dance, drink, and mess around.

"Miss Dolores is nice to me," I had said. "She must be a good Christian."

"I don't know about that," Mama had snorted. "But working in a place like that isn't a decent way for a woman to make a living."

Maybe Mama was right, but Miss Dolores had

prettier clothes than Mama did, and she always seemed happier than Mama, too.

"What you young ladies up to?" Miss Dolores asked as we came up on the porch.

"Carissa need her dress washed," Poppy told her. "She got grapes all over it."

"I can see that," Miss Dolores noted. "You are a sight, girl. You, too, Poppy."

"If her mama sees, Carissa gon' catch it good."

"We don't want that to happen. Let's see what we can do."

Their cabin was a lot like ours inside, except that Poppy had her own cot in the main room. Miss Dolores used the other room for herself. The front room had a cook stove like ours, a table, and three chairs, along with Poppy's bed, plus a dresser and a sideboard. There were things piled up and stuck every which way and on every surface, whether they belonged there or not. Dishes, pots and pans, a hairbrush, jars of pomade and powder, a red skirt that was halfway hemmed, scraps of cloth, scissors, clothes waiting to be washed—Mama would rather die than let *our* place get into such a state.

But on the table, in the middle of the mess, stood a blue glass jar full of yellow goldenrod, arranged just so. I liked it.

Much quicker than I would have thought possible, Miss Dolores got hot, sudsy water into the washtub. Poppy and I both sat in our drawers while our filthy dresses were scrubbed, rinsed, and squeezed out.

Poppy was sent to hang them to dry, and when she came back, Miss Dolores let us put on two of her old dresses. She pinned up the hems and we pranced around the room, pretending to be fine ladies.

Poppy tired of that first and asked if we could go down to the creek.

"Not in those get-ups," Miss Dolores said. "They's old, but they can still do me in a pinch. Lord only knows what kind of state they'd be in once you got 'em down into that creek mud. Y'all can jus' wear your drawers. Ain't nobody gon' be down there. Go on now, and have fun. Jus' don't get wet. Then Carissa'd have to explain how her undies got soaked while her dress stayed dry. Her dress be done before too long."

"Watch out for cottonmouths," I warned as we made our way along the path toward the creek.

"Why you always say that? Ain't no cottonmoufs round here."

"Mama says anytime there's water, there's snakes."

Poppy wasn't convinced. "Your mama ever see a cottonmouf?"

"No . . ."

"You?"

"No . . ."

"Well, then," Poppy said.

Still, I let her lead the way. *She* could be the one to step on the poisonous snake she said wasn't there.

At the creek, we took a long time walking around

in the shallows where the warm water ran clear over pale sand. Down to our left, where the creek curved around a bend, the water deepened into a shadowy green pool. Just where snakes would live, I thought.

Poppy bent over, peering into the water. Her hand darted down and she came up with a crawfish. "Gotcha!" she cried.

I went over for a look. We'd caught lots of crawfish in our time. We'd play by holding twigs in front of them to see if they'd nip at them with their miniature claws. "He's a big one," I said.

"Hold him."

I took him behind his head with my thumb and first finger. He didn't seem happy about it, judging from the way he squirmed. His shell was muddy brown and smooth as a piece of glass. I held another finger in front of him and let him grab at it. He gave me a good pinch that left a mark when he let go.

"My mama says that way over in N'awlins they eat crawfish," Poppy declared knowledgeably.

"You mean New Orleans," I corrected her. "I'm going to let him go."

He was glad to be free, judging from how fast he swam away.

"Let's swim," Poppy said. "It way hot."

"We'll get our drawers wet."

"Take 'em off! I'm gon' down in that deep and cool off."

"Don't," I warned as she began tugging off her

drawers. "Your mama said not to. Besides, that water is deep, and you can't swim."

"C'mon!"

"Snakes live down there. Maybe snapping turtles, too."

Poppy rolled her eyes, but she pulled her drawers back up. "You never want to do nothin'."

"That's not true. I just don't want to get my toe bitten off by a giant turtle."

"Let's go, then. See if our dresses dry."

They were, and Miss Dolores said it was time for me to be getting home.

It wasn't true, what Poppy said about my not wanting to do anything. I liked to do lots of things—just not in the tops of trees or in deep green pools of water. Still, Poppy had claimed she could see all the way to Swainsboro from our magnolia tree. I had no way to know if that was true.

Mama's friend Alma was sitting with Mama on the porch, cutting the ends off okra. The fuzz gave Mama an itchy rash, but Alma said it didn't bother her and she was glad to help out.

"Your mama gon' batter and fry up a batch of this in a little while," she told me as I came up the steps. "Have it with some corn bread and white beans. Mmm, mmm!"

After Mama, Alma was my favorite grownup. I was supposed to love Granma more, but she made it hard sometimes, always fussing about things. Alma, on the other hand, liked everything I did. She said that one day I was going to amount to something and make everyone proud.

"'Afternoon, Miss Alma," I said.

"You been down at Poppy's, I hear."

"Yes, ma'am."

"And how is Zillah?"

"Fine."

"What'd you do at Poppy's?" Mama asked.

"Played at the creek," I said truthfully.

"You watched out for snakes, I hope."

"Yes, ma'am."

"They worry me so," Mama told Miss Alma.

"Poppy's mama makin' it all right?" Miss Alma asked.

"Yes, ma'am. She was sitting on the porch taking it easy."

"When she ought to be cleanin' up that place," Miss Alma declared.

"You're right about that," Mama agreed.

"She have on a new dress?" Miss Alma asked.

"It was pink. With ruffles."

Mama shook her head. "Dressed up for a party in the middle of a workday afternoon. I just don't know."

"Is Mr. Bailey home?" I asked.

"Your mama has been tellin' me all about him," Miss Alma said. "I look forward to meetin' him."

"Guess how Alma heard about that Bailey being here?" Mama said. "Delia Washington! She's been up and down this road all day spreading the news. That woman must think she's a newspaper."

"She sure do love her gossip," Miss Alma added. "Still, Lorena, folks gon' find out about him soon enough."

"There won't be anything to tell, because he's not staying."

"Here he comes," I said.

Bailey braked to a stop and climbed off his bicycle. "'Evenin', everybody. How y'all doin'? How you, Carissa?"

"Mr. Bailey, this is my friend Alma Johnson," Mama said.

"Mighty pleased to make your acquaintance. You two ladies are the prettiest sight I seen all day. Does me a world o' good jus' to look at you, sittin' there like a calendar picture. Where do you stay, Miz Johnson?"

"Up the road, near Rachel."

"Nice to have you so close by. I know that missuz must appreciate havin' a good friend so near."

"You'll have to meet my husband, Ronnie Ray," Miss Alma told him. "I bet you two would have a lot to talk about."

"You married?"

"Married, two children, and a grand-baby."

"That's mighty fine," Bailey said. "Family's the most important thing they is."

Mama got to her feet. "If we're going to eat tonight,

it's time to get on it. Carissa, come and help. Alma, are you done with that okra?"

"Reckon I'll wash up and bring in some wood. Miz Alma, a pleasure to meet you." Bailey tipped his hat and walked his bicycle around the side of the cabin.

Miss Alma waited a minute, as if to be sure Bailey was gone. "You got yourself a prize there," she told Mama. "A real gentleman. I wouldn't be quick to get rid of him."

"I'm so glad everybody knows my business better than I do," Mama retorted.

"Here's the okra. I gotta get home and put Ronnie Ray's supper on the table."

After supper, Bailey repaired the gate. Later, I watched him eat the rest of the scuppernongs. He offered to share them with me, but I didn't want to see another grape for a long time.

Four

Bailey disappeared on his bicycle the next morning and returned in the evening with a roll of chicken wire over the handlebars. He cut wire, hammered, and had the henhouse repaired by my bedtime. Nothing was going to get in and kill Mama's three remaining chickens. I almost wished they *were* all gone; cleaning out the henhouse and feeding the birds were my chores. So was collecting eggs, what few there were. I hated that the most. The chickens didn't like giving them up. They would flap around and peck at my arms. I would grumble to Mama about it, and she'd remind me how much I liked a fried egg once in a while.

Mama thanked Bailey for the repairs and cooked him two eggs for supper. She said he had earned them. "I just hope he didn't steal that wire," she said that night. "All I'd need is to have the sheriff on us for keeping a criminal."

Next morning, when Bailey was getting ready to go to Granma's to fix her porch, I asked him where he got the wire.

"Your mama thinks I stole it," he guessed.

"Did you?" I asked.

"'Course not. I rode to Summit and got me a day job. Traded work for the wire."

"What did you do?"

"Unloaded a truck and stacked lumber at the hardware store. The regular man is down with a bad back."

"How'd you find it?"

"A man who wants to work can usually find somethin' to do if he don't mind what kind o' work he does and ain't afraid to work hard."

"I'll tell Mama."

"*You* didn't think I stole it, did you?"

"No, sir. But Mama doesn't trust people."

"Maybe I can earn her trust, too." He gathered up some tools and turned to go.

"Where'd you get those?"

"Stole 'em," he said simply.

"Mr. Bailey!"

He started to laugh, and then I did, too.

"They're mine," he explained. "I've bought 'em here

and there over the years. By the way, what do *you* do?"

I wasn't sure what he meant. "Do?"

"Besides help your mama and watch Poppy get into trouble."

"I go to school, when it starts."

"You like school?"

I nodded. "Mama says it's important. She says it's the only way I'll ever get out of here, get my education, and become a teacher or something."

"Your mama's right." He arranged his tools in a leather belt he'd pulled out of his pack. Then, "Can you read, Carissa?"

"Of course. I'm twelve, and I've been going to school for six years."

"Wish *I* could."

"You can't *read?*"

"No, child. Never went to no school. Wanted to, though."

"I can show you my books," I told him.

Granma couldn't read, either, but she said she didn't care—except she wished she could read the Bible. Mama could, of course, and had books of her own, but the only one of mine she liked was the one with Bible stories. Mama wouldn't even look at *My Adventures on the Seven Seas* anymore. She said we'd read it together so often that she knew it by heart, and enough was enough.

"I'd like to see them books," he said. "Maybe this evenin' you can show 'em to me."

All day I looked forward to it. When he returned at

suppertime, Granma was with him, decked out in her Sunday best, and he was carrying her picnic basket. I ran inside to tell Mama.

"Granma's all dressed up. How come?" I asked. "Did somebody die?"

"Not that I heard about. Maybe somebody's sick and she's going to make a visit."

"But she doesn't change clothes to do that."

Mama clapped the lid onto the pot of turnip greens. "I know what it is. She has her cap set for that Bailey!"

"What does *that* mean?"

"It means she's flirting with him."

I hadn't paid any attention that first morning when Granma and Mama talked about Bailey going up to live at Granma's, or about Granma and Bailey getting together. The idea had seemed impossible. But now . . .

Before we could say another word, there was Granma at the door. "'Evenin' y'all," she said. "Mister Bailey gone to wash up. Feels lak it's a bit cooler, don't it?"

"You're mighty dressed up for the middle of the week," Mama noted dryly. "Is somebody dead?"

"Not dat I hear tell of."

"Sickness in the preacher's family?"

"No."

"Did all your other clothes burn up?"

"Granma, you smell good," I put in.

"You do for a fact, Miz Rachel," Mama added. "That isn't *perfume,* is it?"

"And she's wearing rouge and lipstick," I exclaimed. "Granma, you look beautiful."

"It's not Sunday," Mama said slowly, "and you aren't going to make a mercy call. I guess that leaves just one other reason you're all tricked out. You and Bailey must be courting. I guess we better call the preacher and reserve the church."

I could tell from her tone that Mama was teasing, but Granma didn't seem to think anything was funny.

"We ain't courtin'," Granma insisted. "Can't a lady look her best once in a while? Lord, I gets so tired o' mah regular clothes, I don't know what to do."

"Where'd you get that paint and cologne?"

"Had 'em. It's time to be usin' 'em, too. I ain't a bad-lookin' woman, an' I ain't in my grave yet."

"You're sweet on Bailey," Mama chirped. "Why, I never thought I'd see the day."

"Yuh mind yo' manners! I said dere ain't nothin' between him an' me, and dere ain't."

"All right," Mama said. "I'm sorry. To what do we owe the honor of your visit?"

"I brought yuh a grape pie an' some fresh-ground cornmeal. Thought maybe I'd get invited fer supper— or ain't I supposed to show mah face round here 'less dey's work I can help with?"

"I am sorry," Mama said, and this time she sounded like she meant it.

I had been enjoying watching Mama tease Granma,

but I didn't want Mama to hurt her feelings. Maybe Granma did like Bailey.

"Of course you're welcome, Miz Rachel," Mama said. "Carissa, set another place."

"Didn't yuh expect Bailey?" Granma asked. "I sees only two plates."

"Bailey eats on the porch."

"Yuh still treatin' him like he's a field hand? Makin' him eat in de yard? He have to come to yo' back door every time he want somethin'?"

"That's not fair," Mama retorted. "My neighbor has a busy tongue, and I have a reputation to uphold. I said from the first that no man is coming into my house while Carissa and I are here alone."

"You ain't alone tonight. I's here. Set two more plates, Carissa."

Mama sighed. "Do as you're told, Carissa. If people are going to gossip, they're going to gossip, and there's not a thing I can do about it."

"Now you talkin' sense," Granma agreed. "Let me get de pie."

The second she turned away from us, Mama caught my eye. Her jaw was set and her mouth was a tight line, but she looked, somehow, as though she'd just as soon laugh out loud as scream with frustration.

There was a knock on the back door. "Let de man in," Granma told me.

"'Evenin', missuz," Bailey said. "My, don't it smell good in here. Sweet potatoes?"

"Yes. Everything will be done in a minute."

"Don't Miz Rachel look good this evenin'?" he said. "This road is jus' full of pretty ladies. Miz Alma, Miz Rachel, you—"

"Don't you try to sweet-talk *me*," Mama warned, "because you're wasting your breath. Carissa, put the biscuits on the table. We're ready to eat."

After supper, Bailey offered to help with the dishes, but Granma wouldn't let him. He sat in one of the rocking chairs on the porch and smoked his pipe while we cleaned up. Then we joined him. Granma took the other rocker and Mama and I sat on the top step. Granma was right about the weather; it was a little cooler. A breeze stirred the leaves at the top of the magnolia tree.

I asked if Bailey could look at one of my books. Mama agreed, so I fetched *My Adventures on the Seven Seas* and brought out a three-legged stool.

"I am so tired of that book," Mama complained. "I'll be glad when school starts and you can get something different."

"May I read some to Bailey?" I asked.

"Some. Just not the part about when the first mate gets his hand cut off."

That was my favorite part of Mr. Armstrong's book, and I used to make Mama read it to me almost every night. She said she couldn't understand how anyone enjoyed such a nasty story.

I sat down next to Bailey and began to read aloud.

When it was dark, I put down *My Adventures on the Seven Seas*. "Have you ever seen the ocean?" I asked Bailey. "I haven't."

"She wears me out, asking about the ocean," said Mama.

"I've seen it," he said. "Couple of times."

"Tell me about it," I begged.

"Isn't it time for you to be in the bed?" Mama said.

"It's only just dark. Can't Mr. Bailey tell me what the ocean is like?"

"Let him, Lorena," Granma chimed in.

"Oh, all right. If it doesn't take too long."

"I first saw the ocean right here in Georgia," Bailey began. "Had to take a boat over to one of the Sea Islands to get there."

"Take a boat to *get* to the ocean?" I asked.

"Uh-huh. In lots o' places here in Georgia, they ain't no other way."

"Why did you go?"

"Heard they was some work. Got a man to take me over in his fishing boat. Found work, cuttin' timber and loadin' it onto barges. You should see the big ol' oak and pine trees they got on those islands. Anyway, on my day off, I decided I'd go look at the ocean."

"It wasn't right there where you were working?"

"Them's some big islands," Bailey told me. "If you didn't know the ocean was nearby, you wouldn't even guess it.

"That first Sunday, I got up early, packed up a

lunch, and headed straight toward the rising sun. First I had to walk through a thick forest. Oak trees, covered in that moss."

"Spanish moss. Miss Johnson says that's its name."

"Spanish moss," Bailey agreed. "Walked through a thick forest, lots o' mosquitoes everywhere. Hot, too. Not a breath o' air stirring. Then the forest ended, and there was this wide, flat plain. No trees, jus' lots o' tall grasses and scrubby little bushes. All sand. I went across that, the sun blazin' down, toward this line o' tall hills straight to the east."

I had read about those hills. "Sand dunes," I said.

Bailey nodded. "Got to the dunes, where they was more thick trees, and climbed up and over. When I came down on the other side, there it was—the ocean."

"What was it like?"

"Big—so big. A monstrous wide, flat beach o' brown sand between me and the water, which was green, not blue like I'd heard it was. Wind blowin' in my face, and a good, clean smell in my nose."

"What about the waves?"

"Tall waves, comin' in fast and heavy. They make a sound like nothin' else I've ever heard—jus' a *whoosh* and a sizzle when the water runs up on the sand, like bacon fryin' in a pan."

That surprised me. "Bacon in a pan?"

"Yes, ma'am. Don't know any better way to describe it."

"What happened next?"

"I stood there for a minute, then I started runnin' right down toward the water. Got to the edge, where the waves slither up high on the sand, like they was comin' to meet me. I looked up the beach in one direction, not a living soul there. Nor in the other direction, neither. It's jus' me and the ocean, all alone. So I took off my shoes and got my feet wet—"

"Was the water cold?"

"No, indeed. Not in August. Cool but not cold. It felt good under that hot sun. Then know what I did?"

"What?"

Bailey lowered his voice. "I took off *all* my clothes and ran right into that water."

That's just what Poppy had invited me to do two days ago.

"How far did you go?"

"Up to my waist. The waves were still comin' in strong, and I had to duck under 'em to keep from gettin' knocked down. So I splashed around, put my head under, took a big mouthful of that salty water, spit it out. Jus' like a child. Reminded me of playin' in the creek near our cabin when I was a boy, 'cept that ocean could swallow a million creeks."

"You weren't afraid of drowning?"

"Never thought about it."

"Or of something biting you?"

"Crab grabbed my toe. That's all."

"Yuh wouldn't get me into no ocean," Granma announced.

"Me, neither," Mama agreed.

"Why not?" I wanted to know.

"God give us legs to walk on de dry land," Granma said. "We ain't no fish."

"Didn't you ever go in the creek?" I asked.

"Loaded with moccasins," Mama said.

"No, I did not," Granma declared. "Never had no time fer dat stuff. Too much work round de place after mah mama died. Why, by de time I wuz Carissa's age—"

"We know, Miz Rachel," Mama broke in.

I was glad she did. Once Granma got started on the story of how her mama died and left her in charge of a father and brother who couldn't bake a biscuit, make a bed, or iron a shirt, no one else would have a chance to say another word.

Bailey came to the rescue. "When I'd had enough o' playin', I walked along the beach to dry off. That's when I started findin' shells."

"Seashells?" I asked. There were pictures of shells in one of Miss Johnson's books, but I'd never seen a real one. "Starfish?"

"Not starfish. But clams, oysters, and lots o' kinds I don't know the names of. And sand dollars."

"What's that?"

"Well, they're—they're hard to describe. If you wait a minute, I can show you one."

"You've got five minutes," Mama told me. "Then it's the bed."

Bailey went to his shed and came back holding a

small leather pouch. Out of it he took something white and round, about the size of one of Mama's biscuits, but much flatter. "Have a look," he said, putting it into my hand.

It was hard to see in the dusk, but the sand dollar felt light. Its surface was grainy, and when I drew a fingernail across it, it felt like the chalkboard at school. The edge was indented in five places, as if someone had pushed into it with a knife blade.

"Shake it," Bailey said.

Something rattled inside.

"What is it?"

"I'll tell you in a minute. Can you see it good?"

"No. It's too dark."

Bailey struck a match, and I examined the surface. On the slightly rounded side—the top?—I could make out what looked like five petals, joined together at the center by a tiny, perfectly shaped five-pointed star.

"It looks like a flower," I said, "with a star in the center."

"Turn it over."

On the other side, five shapes that looked more like leaves than flower petals also came together at the center. The "leaves" even had what looked like veins.

Bailey handed the sand dollar to Mama.

"What makes the noise inside it?" I asked.

"This," Bailey said, reaching into the pouch and bringing out a tiny white object. He struck a new match so I could see.

It looked like two miniature wings, spread for flight. "It's like a little bird," I exclaimed.

"Let me see," Mama said.

"That was inside the sand dollar?" I asked.

"Not this one. Only way for the little birds to come out is if the sand dollar gets broke. Then the birds can go free."

"It's not really a bird," I observed.

"'Course not. Couldn't say what use it is to the sand dollar. Must be somethin' important, though, else it wouldn't be inside."

I fingered the delicate object and then let it rest in the palm of my hand. "It's nice. The sand dollar, too."

"You wouldn't say that if you could see a livin' one," said Bailey.

"Why not?"

"Livin' sand dollar don't look nothin' like that pretty white thing. Alive, a sand dollar is all covered with green slime. Mossy stuff all over it. I found livin' ones and dead ones that day. It even took me a minute t' realize they was the same things. Waves had carried some live ones way up on the beach. I picked up as many as I could and threw 'em back into the water."

"They didn't bite you?"

"Naw. If they got a mouth, it's so tiny you can't even see it."

"Didn't sting yuh?" Granma asked.

"Naw. They got nothing to sting with."

"Yuh wouldn't get me to touch one," Granma declared.

"They jus' felt a little funny," said Bailey. "Cold and slick. Anyway, I figured they deserved another chance. Strange, ain't it, how an ugly outside can hide somethin' pretty on the inside? You can't see the petals or the star while a sand dollar's alive, but they's there, waitin' to show themselves."

Mama broke in. "You forgot one thing."

"What's that?"

"Maybe those pretty dead ones didn't want to die. They didn't know anything about flowers and petals, or the little white birds inside. What if they just wanted to live?"

"I see your point. They's truth there. But it's true too, ain't it, that sometimes one thing has to die for another thing—a beautiful, free thing—to be born?"

"I know all about death. But I've never known anything beautiful or free to come from it. Only sorrow."

Mama often said gloomy things, like she expected the worst to happen. I guessed it had something to do with Daddy.

"Yes, death is hard," Bailey agreed. "Life, too. But sometimes, missuz, they's real pretty things right under our noses, hidden from us unless we look real hard. But they's there, nonetheless."

I liked Bailey's view better than Mama's.

"Girl, it's time for you to be in the bed," Mama said abruptly.

I gave the little bird back to Bailey. He offered to walk Granma home, and Mama ushered me into the house. After she had tucked me in, she went and sat on the porch. I was still awake when Bailey came back, and I heard him say good night to Mama and walk around toward the shed. Still Mama didn't come in, and as I drifted off to sleep, I could hear the slow sound of the rocker creaking against the dried-out boards of the porch floor.

FIVE

Bailey spent the next morning cutting new shakes to repair our roof and the afternoon mortaring Granma's chimney. In the evening, I asked Mama if I could read to him again. Mama agreed, and from then on, Bailey joined us on the porch every evening after supper. If he had tobacco, he'd light his pipe and smoke. If not, he'd hold the cold pipe in his teeth and rock while I read.

Within about three weeks, Bailey had fixed, patched, tightened, and propped up about everything that needed fixing around our place and Granma's. Every time there was a new job and he didn't have all the materials, he'd go into town and come back at the end of the day with what he needed. Usually he traded work for things like nails, cedar shakes, tin, or wire. He even brought home some whitewash and painted our front fence. Sometimes he got pipe tobacco or a bit of flour, cornmeal, or syrup.

By the middle of October, the cotton had all been picked, and we heard that school was scheduled to begin on the third Monday of the month. That stirred up mixed feelings in me. I was looking forward to seeing my teacher, Miss Johnson, a pretty young colored woman with a college degree from someplace called Fisk University. Sometimes I imagined myself doing her job, teaching children new things and helping them make something of their lives. Mama said that being a teacher was one of the finest jobs a person could have, and she would be proud of me if that's what I chose to do.

School also meant new books to read. Mama was right: Mr. Armstrong's book had gotten boring. I was ready for some new stories.

On the bad side, school meant having to put up with Jeralynn and Etta Mae. They were both a little older than I, and they didn't like me. When Poppy and I were together, they didn't mess with us, but when Poppy didn't show up, which was frequently, they picked on me, Jeralynn especially. During one bad week last year, Poppy missed school because she had a runny nose, and Jeralynn decided I had the worst hair and ugliest ears of anyone in the school. For five days straight she tormented me about them. When I complained to Mama and told her I wasn't going to school anymore, she lectured me on how education was precious, and how Jeralynn was part of the pricetag. I should just ignore her because she was a nasty girl who didn't know better. That was easy for Mama to say but hard for me to do.

On the Saturday afternoon before school was set to begin, we were sitting on the porch while Mama hemmed me a new blue dress. She'd saved enough money to buy some calico at the store so I wouldn't have to go to school in a feed-sack dress. Bailey had come home at noon and was sitting with us. Without warning, Mama said, "Well, Mr. Bailey, you've done about all there is to do around here and at Miz Rachel's. We're mighty grateful to you, but I'm sure you're ready to move on."

I was shocked. Bailey had been with us only a few weeks, but now I couldn't imagine life without him. I'd never known what it was like to have a father or grandfather, but having Bailey around made our family feel complete. Why was Mama asking him to leave?

Bailey didn't look worried. "You's right about one thing, missuz," he began. ("Missuz" was all I ever heard Bailey call Mama.) "The work round here is under control. Place looks pretty good. Of course, stuff can break or wear out any time. But I've been studyin' things out, and I want to ask you a favor."

"What is it?" Mama sounded cautious.

"If you could see clear to let me stay till spring, I'd be obliged."

Until that moment, I hadn't thought about how long Bailey would stay, or if he would ever leave. But now I was sure of one thing: I wanted him to be with us, not just until spring, but forever.

"Till *spring?*" Mama said. "Why?"

"I jus' need a stoppin' place. I walked all over the land for many years, until I discovered that riding a bike is so much easier. Then I came here, and it feels like home. If you'd let me stay, I'd earn my keep like I have been. You do think I've earned my keep, don't you?"

"Well . . . yes," Mama admitted. "We have had some little extra since you've been here, Mr. Bailey." (That was all I ever heard *her* call *him*.) "Your help is much appreciated, but—"

Bailey didn't let Mama finish. "I can keep on doin' day work and still help out round the place," he went on. "Cold weather is comin' soon. I can get firewood for free—from the woods—and save you money."

He was right. In the winter, we needed more wood than ever, since we had to heat the cabin as well as keep up with Mama's laundry work. Last winter Mama had had to pay for a man to bring her wood.

"I want Mr. Bailey to stay," I said. "He helps us."

"I didn't hear anyone ask your opinion," Mama snapped. "You best keep quiet."

Mama's attitude puzzled me. I couldn't see anything wrong with Bailey staying, and Mama seemed to have gotten used to his being around. Why was she changing her mind now?

"Mr. Bailey, I have to be frank," Mama said. "I don't know a thing about you. I don't know where you're from, or where you're headed, or why you stopped here, of all places. As far as I know, you're a fugitive from a chain gang. And when they come get you, I'm going to be in trouble, too."

Bailey laughed so hard his pipe almost fell out of his mouth. "That's the beatin'est thing I ever heard," he said. "'Fugitive from a chain gang'!" Then he got serious. "I've seen chain gangs, though. Plenty of 'em, 'specially in Mississippi. I've seen lots o' things. Saw a man hanged and a woman beaten and driven out of town—"

This was more interesting than anything I'd ever read in a book, better even than Howard Armstrong's mate losing his hand. "Where was that?" I asked. "Tell us about it."

"Hush!" Mama cried. "You don't need to know about that mess. Mr. Bailey, please remember she's just a child."

I wanted to say I was almost thirteen, but one look at Mama told me I should keep quiet.

"Sorry, missuz," Bailey said. "You're right."

"But how *did* you come to see all that?" Mama wondered. "Just who are you, and where are you from?"

"I was born a slave, missuz."

"You were?" I asked. "What was it like?"

There were still some old people on Canoochee

Road who had been slaves a long time ago, but I never heard them talk about it. Mama wouldn't let me ask any questions, either. She said it was something that colored folks wanted to forget.

"Didn't I tell you to hush?" Mama warned me. "One more word, and you're going to sit in a corner inside the house. You hear me?"

"Yes, ma'am." I promised myself I wouldn't open my mouth. I wanted to hear what Bailey would say.

"Go on, Mr. Bailey," Mama said. "Carissa won't interrupt you again."

He looked at me, and a twinkle in his eye let me know *he* wasn't annoyed.

"I was born a long way from here, over near Albany," Bailey said. "I was jus' a baby when the war ended. My folks had been slaves together, and when they got free, they stayed together with me and nine of my brothers and sisters. After the war, we sharecropped. I sho' did hate that. Stayed as long as I could stand it, until I was in my twenties, then told Ma and Pa I had to take off. That was back in the eighties, I reckon. I hit the road jus' like I'm doin' now. Goin' from one place to another, findin' work, stayin' one place awhile, then movin' on. Got married in Alabama and settled down. My wife had our baby girl, too."

"What happened then?" Mama asked, as Bailey lapsed into silence.

"They . . . died."

"How?" I asked before I could stop myself.

"You don't have to answer," Mama told him. I waited for her to send me inside the house, but she didn't.

Bailey gazed across the road toward the pine woods. "Fever," he replied. He paused. "That's somethin' I don't much like talkin' about." Then he changed the subject. "I've worked the railroads—that's how I got up north. You ever see snow?" he asked me.

"A little," I said. "Two winters ago."

"We had a cold December," Mama added. "It snowed a bit two days before Christmas."

Bailey nodded. "I've seen snow, seen rivers and ponds hard with ice. Been to New York and Boston and Washington. Traveled through Virginny, the Carolinas, cut timber on the Georgia Sea Islands, like I told you. Even been to Florida and picked oranges."

The more Bailey talked, the more I wished I could see the things he'd seen. My books told me there was a big world beyond mine, and Mama kept promising we'd escape Summit one day and see some of it. In the meantime, Bailey could at least tell me about it. I was sure he had lots of wonderful stories, but I'd never get to hear them if Mama sent him away.

"You never get tired of moving?" Mama asked.

"I'm tired now. That's why I want to stay here this winter. The road gets too long sometimes, and I need a rest."

"Well, . . ." Mama began.

"Please say that Mr. Bailey can stay," I said. Once again I had broken my promise to keep quiet. I started to get up, certain that Mama would send me inside this time. Instead, she motioned to me to be still.

"You promise you aren't a runaway criminal?" Mama asked.

He shook his head.

"You're not one of those men with wives and children in every state?"

He smiled and shook his head again.

Was Mama about to give in? Maybe. At least Bailey's answers seemed to satisfy her. I strained to find another reason why he should stay. "Mr. Bailey can teach me how to ride his bicycle. And he can help with things, just like he's been doing," I added for good measure.

"You don't know how to ride?" he asked, surprised. "I thought every child— Why didn't you ask me to show you?"

"I didn't want to tell the truth," I admitted, hanging my head and looking as pitiful as I could. "Would you teach me? Poppy wants to learn, too." Poppy hadn't said a word about it, but I knew she'd want to if she had the chance. I turned pleading eyes upon him, praying my performance would persuade Mama.

"Are you still going to earn your keep?" she asked him.

"Word of honor. I can always find things to do round town. If white men don't feel like payin' with cash money, they pay with goods. Somehow that don't feel the same to 'em as givin' a colored man cash."

"You don't need to tell me about the ways of white folks. They want the most they can get out of you while giving back the least. They'll lie to you, cheat you, and treat you like a dog."

I'd often heard this speech from Mama. Granma and Miss Alma agreed with her, too. As far as I knew, they were right. I didn't see many white people, except for the ladies Mama worked for. They seemed nice enough, but Mama said their niceness hid their true selves. When it came down to it, they'd do you dirt every time.

"I reckon that's true about some of 'em," Bailey replied, "but I've known some mighty decent white folks, too. They's jus' like us, really. Some of 'em are deep down good, and some deep down mean."

Maybe it was just the white people in Summit who were wicked. Maybe Mama was wrong about the rest of them.

"Most of them are mean," Mama declared. "Lots of colored folks, too. I sometimes wonder how the world got to be so full of hateful people."

"It's hard to see the good sometimes, but it's there. You jus' gotta look for it."

Mama didn't answer.

"Anyway, if I stay, I'll make certain you have enough meal, flour, coffee, sugar—jus' tell me what you need."

Mama didn't reply, but I could almost see her mind working. We had had a hard time last winter, with nothing from our own garden except turnips, collards, and sweet potatoes, and nothing much besides the usual corn bread, beans, eggs, and a little pork. Maybe with Bailey's help, there could be some extras—like fresh oranges.

"All right, Mr. Bailey. You can stay if it doesn't cost me anything. And I want you to teach Carissa to ride your bicycle."

"You got yourself a deal. I 'preciate it."

I offered Mama my most grateful look, but she just gave a little "hmmph" and went back to her hemming.

In bed that night, I asked Mama again why she was so suspicious of Bailey. "He just wants to help us," I told her.

"How do you know that? As far as I can make out, nobody in this world does anything for free. Everybody wants something. That Delia Washington wanted to know my business, and those scuppernongs were the price she was willing to pay. Mr. Bailey wants something, too, and I wish to heaven I could figure out what it is. Carissa, I've told you and told you that you can't trust anybody, except maybe your own family."

"I trust Bailey."

"That's what you've been saying since the moment he arrived. Are you still going on that spooky feeling of yours?"

"Yes, but Bailey's done a lot of things for us, too. He's proved that he's a good man!"

"Then you've got a lot to learn. He comes here, acts all interested in us, does a few chores, sits on the porch evenings, lets you read to him, and suddenly you trust him."

"Why shouldn't I?"

Mama finished undressing, got into bed beside me, and turned out the oil lamp.

"Because you never know what people might do. Or what they might be."

"I don't understand."

"Of course you don't. You're too young to know how cruel this world can be. Let's just hope you aren't wrong about Mr. Bailey and that I'm not a fool for letting him stay."

Mama got quiet, and I lay there thinking. Bailey's wife and little girl—what was her name?—had died. That must have hurt him a lot; I knew what my daddy's death had done to Mama.

Then my thoughts turned to something else Bailey had said. "Mama, you weren't ever a slave, were you?"

"Good Lord, girl! No. I'm too young. Besides, I'm from the North. They got rid of their slaves long before they did down here. What put that idea into your head?"

"I don't know. Was Granma a slave? She's from the South, and she's old."

"You better not say that in front of *her*. No, your granma is too young, too. Slavery ended in 1865, and Granma wasn't born until 1870. Her parents were slaves, though."

"Bailey was born a slave. He said so."

"I heard him. I was there, remember? That means he was born before 1865."

"Were all colored people in America slaves once?"

"No. There have always been some free colored people, North and South. There were slaves in the North at first, but like I told you, they were freed when the states passed laws saying so. Those states did it on their own, without being forced. The southern states held on to their slaves until they were made to give them up. The Civil War saw to that."

"What's it like to be a slave?"

"How should I know?"

"Miss Johnson said that slaves were beaten. She said they couldn't get married or live together in families the way we can now. They couldn't own their own land and could be bought and sold like animals."

"Miz Johnson had better watch what she says to you children. She'll get herself into a mess of trouble if certain white folks find out."

"She said that slaves couldn't live where they wanted or move when they wanted."

"I guess I do know something about it, after all," Mama muttered.

"Why did people own slaves? Miss Johnson said that slave masters were cruel and—"

"Stop now! Haven't I got enough troubles without having to answer questions about all that mess?"

"No one can make us slaves again, can they?"

"Didn't I just say—" Mama stopped herself. "No,

sugar, no one can make us slaves again. And one day, after you have your education, you move away from here, go back north, and you'll be safe."

"Aren't I safe now?"

"No more questions. I need my rest, and so do you."

With that, Mama kissed me on the cheek, gave me a hug, and turned on her side. Soon, her breathing told me she was asleep.

I lay awake for a long time. Lots of different things swirled in my mind. Lots of questions. What was it like to be a slave? Why was it so hard for Mama to trust anyone? There were two things I knew for certain, though. She was wrong about Bailey, and I was right.

It was a scary feeling, going against what Mama said. For my whole life, I'd believed what she told me, and I'd never known her to be wrong. If she was wrong about Bailey, then she could be wrong about other things, too. Like about all white people being mean.

Mama often told me I had to think for myself. Maybe she didn't expect that when I did, I might come up with an idea different from hers.

❧

That night a cold front came through, and next morning was the first really chilly one we'd had in months. I pulled the sheet up around my neck and nestled in close to Mama to keep warm. Then she got up and splashed water on her face, and I heard her say, "My, that's like ice."

After church and dinner, Bailey invited Poppy and me to come learn how to ride the bicycle. Poppy was ready—she was *always* ready for anything new—but suddenly I wasn't so sure. The thought of falling off and breaking my bones got me wondering if I really wanted to do it.

Bailey stood in the road, holding the bike upright. "Who wants to go first?" he asked.

"I do!" Poppy exclaimed. She scrambled up onto the seat and grabbed the handlebars. "Come on," she urged. "Let's go."

"Whoa! You gotta put your feet on the pedals."

Poppy's legs weren't long enough to reach, so Bailey had her get off while he lowered the seat. When he'd made the adjustment, she climbed back on. "I'm ready," she announced.

"I reckon you are," he agreed. "Now, you start pedalin', and I'm gon' trot alongside of you and hold you so you won't fall over."

"Let's go!"

Bailey held on to the bicycle, and they started down the road. At first they went slowly, but when Poppy began to pedal faster, Bailey had to run to keep up. "Faster!" Poppy ordered. "Now let go." He did, and Poppy shot ahead. She sped along for a few moments, wobbling from side to side. How easy it looked! That gave me confidence. But then she crashed onto her right side. I was horrified, but she came up laughing. "Again!" she declared.

"You're not hurt?" I asked, running up to her.

"Nope! Come on, Mr. Bailey. Again!"

They started slowly, sped up, Bailey let go, and Poppy rode for a few seconds and then fell over. Like the first time, she jumped up and asked for another chance. Again Bailey got her going, and again she fell. This happened half a dozen times, but each time she went farther before she crashed. The last time, Poppy came up with a scraped and bleeding knee, but she just wiped the blood away and asked for another turn.

"Carissa next," Bailey told her. "You done real good, though. Won't take much more for you to get it. Ready?" he asked me.

I looked at Poppy's bloody knee.

"It fun," Poppy assured me. I couldn't hang back now. Not in front of Poppy. Not after telling Mama that Bailey had to stay so he could teach me to ride.

"Get on," he told me. I climbed on while he held the bicycle steady. The seat was too low for me, so I got off, and Bailey raised it. I hoped Poppy saw that I was a good bit bigger than she, despite what Miss Dolores said. When the bike was ready, I got on again. "Now, put your feet on the pedals," Bailey said, "and we'll begin jus' the way you saw me do with Poppy. Your job is to pedal, and I'm gon' hold on to you while you find your balance."

"Find my balance?"

He thought for a second. "It's hard to explain. But you'll know when it happens. You find it when you can ride by yourself and feel like the ground on either side ain't gon' reach up and pull you down. You'll see."

I started to pedal and we started to move. I was holding the handlebars as tightly as I could. "Don't let go!" I shouted as we picked up speed.

"Keep pedalin' and aim straight."

Down the road we went, Bailey puffing with exertion, me gripping the bars for dear life. "Don't let go," I kept saying. And he didn't.

"Slow down!" he said at last.

"How?"

"Put on the brakes!"

"How?"

But Bailey was breathing too hard to give me an answer, so I just took my feet off the pedals. Fortunately, he was able to pull the bike to a stop and keep me from falling. He was gasping for air, and I was wet with perspiration, more from fear than anything.

"Good girl," Bailey said, panting. "You're doing fine."

"I am?"

"Yes, ma'am. Soon as I get my wind back, we'll go again."

After Bailey had rested, we tried it again. When we were going pretty fast, I felt Bailey give me a little extra push, heard him say, "Now pedal hard," and felt him let go.

"Go, Carissa!" Poppy shouted.

The second he let go, I crashed over into the road.

Bailey and Poppy hurried to where I lay in the dirt, humiliated. "You hurt?" he asked. I pointed to my right forearm, which stung like fury. "You're fine," he pronounced, helping me to my feet.

"I knew this would happen," I said, trying hard not to cry. "I don't like it, and I can't do it."

"'Course you can. You ain't given it a chance yet. Let's try again."

"Don't be a scaredy-cat," said Poppy. I wanted to push her down.

"I can't do it," I repeated.

"You ain't gon' give up, are you?" asked Bailey. "A brave girl like you?"

I didn't feel brave, and I hated the bicycle lying in the road, all spotted now with red Georgia dust.

"You did fine. Nobody does it the first time. That balance thing is hard to find."

"Go on," Poppy urged. "You can do it."

"I can't!"

"Hard to find," Bailey went on. "But once you find your balance, Carissa, you ain't never gon' lose it."

"How do you know?"

"Everybody says so. It's like knowin' how to read."

"What do you mean?"

"Did you always know how to read?"

I shook my head.

"Your mama and your teachers had to teach you, right?"

"Uh-huh."

"But now you know how. And you ain't never gon' forget, are you?"

"No . . ."

"'Course you ain't. You're gon' know how to read till your dyin' day. Once you know it, you know it. Ridin' a bicycle is the same thing. After you learn how, you never forget."

"Maybe I'll try again tomorrow."

"Now's as good as tomorrow. Better. Besides, don't school start tomorrow?"

"Yes."

"Then let's go. Your time is gon' be taken up later. Besides, I got me a full-time job yesterday, and beginning tomorrow I ain't gon' be round as much."

"A job? Where?"

"Hardware store where I've been workin'. Man who worked there hurt his back, like I told you. Well, he didn't get better and didn't get better, so Mr. Satterwhite had to let him go. Hired me full-time yesterday."

"What will you do?"

"All kinds o' stuff. Sweep, take out trash, load lumber, carry orders to folks' trucks. Whatever needs to be done."

"It's three miles to Summit."

"So? This ol' bicycle will get me there in no time. Now, let's go."

I didn't want to, but I couldn't find an excuse that didn't make me sound like a baby. And I wasn't going to let Poppy think I was a scaredy-cat.

Bailey patted the seat, and I got on. He kept a firm hand on the bicycle, and this time I began to feel that at least I had control over where it was headed. I didn't fall. On our third trip, Bailey warned me he was going to let go and let me try again to find my balance. I grabbed the handlebars tightly and nodded that he could release me. I managed to ride alone for a short way before I fell over again.

Bailey ran to me, shouting, "You balanced! Did you feel it? For a moment you was balancin'. How was it?"

Poppy was right behind him. "You doin' good!"

I had bloodied my elbow this time. I got to my feet, again trying not to cry. "Did I really balance?" I asked, peering at my elbow.

"'Deed you did. You're gon' get it. Want to try again?"

"No, sir."

Bailey didn't argue. He walked us to the house and turned me over to Mama, who had been watching from the front door.

I held out my arm. "I'm cut," I announced.

"Me, too!" Poppy added, proudly displaying her knee.

"Let me have a look." Mama inspected our scrapes. "Hmm . . . You two will live. Let me put on some iodine."

"Just soap. Not iodine." I hated how it stung.

Mama ignored me. She sat Poppy down on the porch and fetched a damp cloth and the iodine bottle. "When was the last time you had a bath?" she asked, dabbing at Poppy's knee. "I can barely find the skin underneath this layer of dirt."

"Mama say she gon' wash me good tonight for school tomorrow."

"I hope you decide to study hard this year. What's going to become of you without an education?"

"I dunno," Poppy said airily.

"Girl, you'd better start thinking about your future."

"Aw, missuz, a child her age can't think that far ahead," said Bailey. "She's too busy enjoyin' life."

"Then her mama ought to think about it for her. At least make the child attend school every day. A woman who doesn't want something better for her child isn't much of a mother."

"I can do what I want when I grow up," Poppy announced. "Mama says so."

"Good luck, then. Because *you* are going to *need* it." Mama finished cleaning Poppy's knee and applied the iodine. Poppy never flinched. "You're done," she told her.

Then she doctored me. The iodine stung, but I wasn't going to make a fuss, not in front of Poppy and Bailey.

He told us we were the bravest girls he knew. Then he said it was time to clean the bicycle.

"You two go help," Mama added, offering a soft rag that had once been part of a bed sheet. "Use this."

We followed Bailey to the back yard and helped

wash and dry the bicycle. Then he picked up the cloth Mama had sent. "Jus' what I need for the polish."

"Polish?"

"Got to shine her up after she's washed. This will do the trick." He reached for a little jar beside the water bucket.

"Can we help?"

"Be glad for you to."

So Bailey applied the polish and Poppy and I rubbed the frame and fenders until they gleamed. When we were done, we stepped back and admired the result.

"Looks good as new, don't it?" Bailey asked.

"But it's getting scratched," I said. "From when Poppy and I fall off."

Bailey patted the handlebars tenderly. "Don't you worry none about that. Everythin' shows some wear an' tear sooner or later. Only way to keep somethin' perfect is never to use it. And *that* ain't any fun. No, if we take good care of her, this ol' bike will give good service for a long time to come."

It was easy to see why Bailey loved his bicycle. It had apparently helped him visit lots of interesting places and see amazing things. Maybe learning to ride a bicycle could do the same for me. At that moment, though, I didn't much feel like trying. In fact, I was afraid. And I wondered—could I ever learn to ride without falling and cutting up my elbow, or something even worse?

Six

That night as I tossed in bed, a pecan fell on our roof—*pong!* Six pecan trees grew in the yard, and this year there would be a good crop. The next time we had wind or rain, the pecans would come down by the bucketfuls and we would pick them up for Mr. Thompson, our landlord. We'd "go halves" with him, splitting the profits from selling the nuts at Hall's store. Then we might have a little extra money for Christmas presents.

Next morning, I hopped out of bed, washed—the water in the basin was cold again—and got into my new school dress. The fabric was crisp against my shoulders and legs, and felt even better than the soft-ness that would come later, after many washings. The shine of the blue cloth pleased me, too—it looked so new. Mama buttoned me and watched me spin around, letting the skirt flare. Then came my new shoes, sturdy brown ones with straps across and gold buckles on the side, smelling like new leather and polish. They were the first pair I'd had since last fall and had to last a long time. I looked down at myself and was satisfied. Mama fixed my hair and gave me a starched white handkerchief to tuck into the belt of my dress. I was ready to go.

"Shall I call Mr. Bailey to eat?" I asked, as Mama dished up grits and fried potatoes.

"He's long gone. Didn't he tell you he got a full-time job?"

"Yes . . ."

"Well, it takes time to get there, even on a bicycle. I heard him leave before you were awake. It would make more sense for him to find a place to live in town."

I didn't want to hear that so soon after Mama had agreed to let him stay with us.

Mama spooned grits onto my plate. "Then he wouldn't have to do all this back-and-forth stuff. Be-sides, we *could* get along without him. A woman has to be able to manage on her own. Don't ever count on anyone to do for you what you can do for your-self."

"Didn't Daddy take care of us, Mama?"

"He tried. But he went off to war when you were still tiny, so how could he help us then except to send us his pay? After he got killed, I had to manage without him. Never lean on somebody else, because you never know when that person might leave you. You have to take care of *yourself*. Understand?"

I wanted to remind Mama that we had moved to Summit because she *couldn't* manage on her own after Daddy died, but I'd learned it was usually better to keep quiet than to contradict her. "Daddy didn't mean to leave us," I said instead.

"I know, sugar. But he left just the same, didn't he?"

"Yes."

"I'm just worried that you'll be all to pieces when Bailey leaves here—"

"He *won't* leave. He wants to stay with us. He fixed everything, and brings extra food—"

"I admit he's done that." Mama sat down across from me. "But we can't let ourselves rely on him, or on anything he does for us. One day, he'll be gone, and we'll have to take care of ourselves, just like we did before he came here. So don't you get too—too dependent on him, for anything."

"He won't leave," I insisted.

"Did he give you that in writing?"

"No—"

"A fortuneteller look into her crystal ball and promise you that?"

"Mama, be serious!"

"I am. I want you to realize that nothing in this life is certain, except that we're all going to die."

This wasn't what I wanted to hear on the first day of school. But maybe it was my fault that Mama was being so gloomy. I was the one who mentioned Daddy, and talking about him always made her sad.

"I'm sorry," she said. "Let's enjoy having Bailey here and not worry about the future. All right?"

"All right."

"Now, eat your breakfast before it gets cold. I'll get your dinner together."

While I ate, Mama wrapped up a sweet potato and some corn bread for me to take. There was a knock on our door, and before I could answer, Poppy burst into the room.

"'Mornin', Miz Lorena, hey, Carissa," she bubbled. "Like my new dress?"

I looked at Poppy in wonder. From the top of her head to the soles of her shoes, she was the most fixed-up I'd ever seen her.

"Your dress is *something*," said Mama. "Brightest pink it can be. Did your mama make it for you?"

"Yes, ma'am. She sewed the ruffles on the collar and hem so it would look jus' like hers."

"She must have done all your pigtails, too." Poppy's head was a mass of tiny neatly braided pigtails, each tied with a bright piece of ribbon.

"Yes, ma'am. Took all evenin' last night."

"And pretty pink socks and new black shoes," Mama noted. "You are a picture."

"Yes, ma'am. You ready, Carissa?" Poppy had a brand-new copybook and two sharpened pencils. Maybe she had listened to what Mama had said about getting an education. Perhaps she would actually try to learn something in school this year.

I gathered up my supplies and my dinner and off we went. Other children were on their way, too, all taking Canoochee Road the mile into the country where the colored children's school was. I saw Etta Mae up ahead, and a little cold knot formed in my stomach. We walked more slowly so that we wouldn't catch up with her.

"She nasty," Poppy declared. "Big ol' cow."

I giggled. Etta Mae *was* plump, and she had the biggest appetite in school. Still, she was popular, and she had already started growing the curves I wished I had.

Etta Mae stopped at Jeralynn's house, and Jeralynn appeared. She looked good, I had to admit. *Her* curves were fully developed already. In fact, she had more than Mama did. Her skin was lighter than mine, and her hair softer and wavier. "Lots of white blood in that family *somewhere,*" Mama had declared. Jeralynn was pretty, but she could be mean as a nest of hornets, and if she didn't like you, she could wreck your day at school.

She came to the gate, greeted Etta Mae, and then

said, just loud enough to make sure Poppy and I both heard her, "Look at that funny little clown comin' along. Circus must be in town."

Poppy dropped her dinner and school supplies and lunged toward Jeralynn. I grabbed her just in time. "Don't," I whispered fiercely. "Don't mind her."

"I'm gon' kill her," Poppy cried. "Let me go!"

"No. She's bigger than you, and Etta Mae is on her side. You don't stand a chance."

"I don't care. She can't do me like that and get away with it."

"You'll ruin your new dress."

"I don't care. Mama can make me another one."

Jeralynn and Etta Mae kept walking. I wanted to give them a big head start.

"Your mama won't make you another one if she finds out you ruined this one fighting," I said to Poppy.

"Who gon' tell her?"

"I am."

Poppy stuck out her tongue at me.

"Don't be a baby. Forget what Jeralynn said and let's go. Miss Johnson won't let her bother you."

Poppy picked up her things. "I don't care 'bout Miss Johnson or nothin'. If that girl mess with me again, I'll get her good."

"Let's go. We don't want to be late."

When we got to school, Jeralynn and Etta Mae were among the rest of the students waiting for Miss Johnson to open the door. Everyone was talking, and some of the smaller children were running around, shouting and teasing. If Jeralynn noticed us, she gave no sign. Perhaps there wouldn't be any trouble.

The door opened and Miss Johnson stepped out. She was wearing a maroon dress with small white polka dots on it. I thought I knew every dress Miss Johnson owned, but I hadn't seen this one before. She must have bought it for the first day of school. At her throat she had pinned her favorite brooch, a cameo that had belonged to her grandmother. It was beautiful. I had promised myself that one day I would have one like it. Miss Johnson's short dark hair was carefully curled and framed her brown face. She was the prettiest lady I knew.

"Good morning, everyone," Miss Johnson said.

"Good morning, Miss Johnson."

"I'm glad to see all of you today." She scanned our faces. "We have some new students with us. That's wonderful. I think we have thirty-six altogether. It's going to be a bit tight inside, but we'll manage, if everyone cooperates and uses good manners. Now, come along, and no pushing."

We filed into the school building through broad double doors. Just inside was a wide, dim room where we could hang our coats in cold weather and leave our dinners in cubbyholes. Poppy and I put our dinners away and went into the classroom, which could be reached through two doors, one at either end of the cloakroom. The classroom was large, but Miss Johnson was right: it would be crowded with thirty-six students. Tall windows on the side walls let in plenty of sunshine on nice days, but when it was cloudy, the room could be gloomy, almost too dark to read in. A wood-burning stove sat in the center, its metal chimney running up through the ceiling.

Poppy and I found seats next to each other, but we knew not to sit down yet. Miss Johnson came into the room last and took her place on the raised platform where her desk stood in front of the blackboard. She led us in prayer and assigned us our seats, and another school year began.

The morning passed, and then it was time for dinner and recess. Outside in the schoolyard, Poppy and I were eating together when Miss Johnson came up to us. "Did you have a good summer, Carissa? That's a very pretty dress, Poppy."

"Yes, ma'am," I answered. "I had a good summer."

"Mama made it for me," Poppy said.

"Promise me you'll come to school every day this year," Miss Johnson told her. "You must learn to read. Carissa will help you if you let her."

"Yes, ma'am." Poppy knew all the right things to say to a grownup.

"Carissa, I have some new books I want you to see," Miss Johnson told me. "I was in Atlanta this summer and picked out several for our school. There is one in particular I think you'll like. It's called *Little Women,* by a New England writer named Louisa May

Alcott. You may take it home with you this afternoon."

"Thank you," I said. Miss Johnson liked me; I knew that. Maybe it was because I never gave her any trouble. I loved her too much to think of doing that. Even if I had thought of it, I would have been afraid to. If Mama ever found out I was acting up in school, I'd get it for sure.

"Let me meet some of our new students," she said. "Remember your promise, Poppy. School every day."

That afternoon, just as school was let out, it started to rain. It had turned cold, too. Poppy and I waited for the rain to let up so we wouldn't get soaked on our way home. After fifteen minutes it was just a fine mist, and we decided to start walking. I put *Little Women* inside my binder, to protect it from the rain. We walked cautiously, trying to avoid puddles and mud holes and keep our shoes dry.

Halfway home, we came up on Jeralynn and Etta Mae, who seemed in no hurry. Just then it began to drizzle again, so Poppy and I had to pass them if we wanted to reach home before we got wet.

I was hoping that Poppy had forgotten Jeralynn's insult from the morning. She hadn't.

As we passed Jeralynn and Etta Mae, Poppy ran toward them, found a puddle, and kicked muddy brown water all over Jeralynn's skirt. "Hog!" she shouted as she darted past.

With a scream, Jeralynn took off after Poppy, with Etta Mae right behind her. I stood where I was, too scared to move. Something terrible was about to happen. I was sure of it.

Poppy was fast, but Jeralynn was faster. She managed to grab Poppy by the back of her dress and pull her down onto the road. Then she began kicking mud on her.

"Get off me, you smelly skunk!" Poppy shouted. "I'm gon' kill you!" She managed to get onto her knees and grab at Jeralynn, but Etta Mae pushed her back.

"Bitch!" Poppy screamed.

Etta Mae and Jeralynn stopped their attack. "What did you call me?" Etta Mae yelled.

"You heard me!" Poppy cried. "You mean ol' hound dogs!"

"Hold her!" Jeralynn ordered. Etta Mae pinned Poppy's shoulders to the ground, and Jeralynn began punching her in the face.

Now I was really frightened. Jeralynn and Etta Mae were going to hurt Poppy badly. She was my friend, and I couldn't let that happen. "Leave her alone!" I shouted. I went for Jeralynn and tried to pull her away from Poppy, but she turned on me. She grabbed my hair and pulled—hard. Then Etta Mae tackled me and threw me to the ground. I went down in a puddle, right next to where Poppy was lying on her back. There was a thin trickle of blood running from her lip.

"You keep your little dog on a leash, you know what's good for you." Jeralynn looked down at me sprawled in the mud. "Come on," she commanded Etta

Mae. "It starting to rain hard." She kicked mud at us one more time and went on her way.

We watched them go. Poppy began to cry, but not from hurt. She was furious.

"Are you all right?" I asked.

She ignored me. "I'll get you!" she shrieked toward Jeralynn and Etta Mae in the distance. "You'll see!"

"You hush! Look at what you did."

We pulled each other up and looked at ourselves. We were both covered with mud, our shoes were soggy, and we were getting soaked. Poppy went back for her copybook, and then I remembered *Little Women*. Where was my binder? When I went to help Poppy, I must have dropped it. "Please, please, please, God, don't let it be in the mud," I prayed.

My binder lay just where I'd been standing when I ran to save Poppy. It was open, and *Little Women* was still inside, getting pelted by the cold rain that was now pouring down on us.

"No!" I cried, scooping up the binder and closing it tight. Miss Johnson's book was wet, but maybe the pages inside had stayed dry. Perhaps it wasn't all ruined. But even so, the damage to the book was worse, much worse, somehow, than everything that had happened to Poppy and me. Miss Johnson had trusted me to take care of *Little Women,* and this was how I repaid her.

"Look what you did!" I cried, shaking my binder at Poppy. "If you hadn't messed with Jeralynn, nothing would have happened."

"I'm sorry," she mumbled.

"C'mon." I began walking, cradling the binder to my chest, its spine facing upward so that the rain couldn't get to *Little Women* more than it already had. I wanted to run, but there was no point now. We couldn't get any wetter than we were.

Poppy caught up with me and took hold of my arm. "I'm sorry," she said again.

"You always make trouble," I grumbled.

"Thank you for savin' me."

"I didn't do anything."

"You made 'em stop."

"I don't want to talk about it anymore."

Mama was waiting for us at the door. As she got us out of our wet clothes, toweled us off, put us in dry drawers, and wrapped us in quilts, we explained what had happened.

Mama was not pleased with Poppy. "You see what your sass got you and Carissa into?" she said. "Your new dress is torn at the collar and stained red with clay, and your shoes are wet enough to wring dry. Why couldn't you ignore that girl? She was just waiting for you to take her bait so she could mess with you. And now see the results."

I knew it served Poppy right to have Mama yell at her, and I wanted to feel glad about it. But Poppy looked so hangdog that I started to feel sorry for her.

"I'm sorry, Miz Lorena. But she say my new dress

make me look like a clown. Ain't nobody gon' talk that way to me."

"And just how do you intend to stop 'em? I promise that wasn't the last time in your life somebody is going to say something that you don't like. You'd better learn to walk away, unless you want a lifetime of fights worse than what you got into this afternoon."

Poppy didn't look convinced.

"Drink this," Mama ordered, giving her a mug of hot tea. "Warm up some so you can get home. I'll bet your mama is worried sick, wondering where you are."

I shivered inside the quilt Mama had wrapped around me, not because I was cold anymore—the fire in the cook stove and the hot tea were making me plenty warm—but because I knew what was going to happen after Poppy left. Mama had noticed the book first thing. I had told her how I had dropped it going to Poppy's rescue, but her expression said that she and I were going to have words.

When Poppy was warm and dry, Mama got her back into her damp clothes and walked her home. I waited, curled inside my quilt, wishing the day had never happened.

Mama came back irritated. "That woman doesn't have the good sense God gave a tick," she announced. "No wonder that child is such a mess."

"What happened, Mama?"

"I got to listen while Poppy told Dolores her sad story, what that Jeralynn said to her this morning and how she tried to get her back this afternoon. And guess what?"

"What?"

"Miz Dolores Toliver said that Poppy was right to go after her! She said she shouldn't let anybody make fun of her. I said, 'What about this girl's dress and new shoes?' and she said, 'I can always make another dress and buy another pair of shoes. I'm glad my little girl thinks enough of her own self that she ain't gon' let nobody talk low-down about her and get away with it.'" Mama looked utterly outraged. "Can you imagine? Saying that in front of a *child*.

"Now, you and I are going to have a talk," Mama continued. "Do you see what it cost you to try to get that girl out of the mess she made for herself? Your new dress is stained, your new shoes are sopping wet, and a brand-new book that your teacher entrusted to you is ruined. We'll have to pay her for it so she can buy a new one. What made you do it?"

"Poppy needed my help," I explained. "I'm older. Isn't it up to me to look after her?"

"That girl is perfectly able to look after herself. Climbing trees, going after a girl a lot bigger than she is! Poppy's not afraid of anything. You should have let her fight it out alone."

"But, Mama, she's my friend. Almost like my sister."

"Don't you think I know that? And, yes, friends are supposed to look out for each other. But you've got to draw the line somewhere. I want you to promise me that the next time something like that happens, you let it be. Let Poppy work out her own mess. When you get involved, there's no telling what might happen to you."

"Mama—"

"That's all I have to say about it. Now, let's see if we can get this book dried out some." She picked it up and looked at the cover. "*Little Women!*" she exclaimed. "I loved this book. I read it when I was about your age."

"I wanted us to read it together," I whispered. That thought had only just occurred to me, but it seemed like a way to get Mama to feel sorry for me.

"That would be nice. To read all about Jo, and Beth, and—oh, there are some funny things in that book. Sad things, too." She opened the soggy book. "Let's see how bad the damage is."

The front cover was soaked and so were the edges of the pages, but most of the inside had stayed dry. It would be readable, Mama said, but the pages would be stained and wrinkled at the edges. We blotted it as best we could, and Mama put it near the fire.

❧

Maybe the upsets of the afternoon had softened Mama's heart, because when Bailey came home at six o'clock, wet and muddy as a catfish pulled from a shallow pond, she asked him into the house for supper. He accepted gratefully.

Bailey went to the shed to change, but he was gone for what seemed a long time. At last, he knocked at the back door.

Mama let him in. "It took you plenty long just to change clothes. Supper's been ready for half an hour."

"Sorry 'bout that. Had to wash and dry my bicycle. Don't want it gettin' rusty, 'specially the chain."

Then he turned to me. I felt fine now—Mama had given me one of her old sweaters to wear. It looked funny, hanging off me, but it felt good. It smelled like Mama, too. I liked that. "How are *you?*" Bailey asked. "How's that first day of school?"

"All right."

"Jus' all right?"

So I told him what had happened, starting with how Jeralynn had insulted Poppy. I told him everything, except the bad word Poppy had used. I hadn't shared that with Mama, either.

Bailey listened, but made no comment except to ask, when I was done, "Now, what you suppose makes one child say somethin' so unkind to another child? Callin' that cute little girl a clown, and her in a brand-new dress, too."

"Some folks are just plain evil," Mama declared. "That Jeralynn acts exactly the way you'd expect her to act, considering her parents. I know them. They think they're so special because they have lighter skin and straighter hair. Or maybe because they've lived on this road for generations. What's so wonderful about being born and growing up in this town that makes folks think they're better than everyone else? Not one of these sorry people has ever been far as Atlanta, let alone Philadelphia, and they act like they're the judge and jury of the whole world. It makes me sick to my stomach to think that any one of those children would look down on anyone else, even Poppy, God help her."

"That corn bread sho' do smell temptin'," Bailey said. "Why don't we talk 'bout this later on?"

"You're right. It's past time for supper. Besides, there's nothing more to say. Carissa, help me dish up the food."

SEVEN

While we ate, Bailey talked and talked, as if trying to get Mama's mind off of my bad day. He told us his day had been pretty good until the afternoon downpour. He'd unloaded two trucks in the rain—by himself, because the man who was supposed to help him had a sudden attack of stomach pains just about the time the storm started.

"Convenient for him, wasn't it," Mama said.

Then Bailey told us about his trip home. The bicycle kept getting stuck in the gooey red mud that turned the dirt roads into what looked like hog wallows. He'd had to give up trying to ride and had walked most of the way.

"That was the least pleasure I've had in anything

for a long time now," Bailey remarked, between spoonfuls of beans. "Usually goin' to work and comin' home are two o' the best parts o' my day."

"Why is that?" I asked.

"Oh, 'cause it's jus' fun to ride. I'm too old to run much anymore, but put a old man on a bicycle, he can fly like a hummin'bird."

"Don't you get weary of going back and forth the same way all the time?" Mama asked. "Lord knows how tired I get of seeing the same trees, same houses, same nosy faces up and down that road."

"Can't say I do," Bailey answered. "Always somethin' new to see. Pokeberries turnin' purple on the bushes, buzzards enjoyin' a possum supper. And folks —always somebody to talk to. I reckon by now I know most o' the families between here and town."

"How? I've been here for years and I don't know all of them. I don't want to, either."

"No special way. I'm ridin' along, they's on their porch or in their yard, and they wave and say 'Hey!' and I wave back and say 'Hey.' Sometimes I stop and we talk a little. Young'uns, they's the most friendly. Can't get enough of lookin' at my bicycle." Bailey got that thoughtful expression I'd learned to recognize. "Come to think of it, that bike o' mine has been the start o' more conversations with more folks than I'd ever thought possible. When I ordered it, I told myself it'd make travelin' a heap easier than walkin'. Never figured it would make me popular, too."

I sat up so suddenly that I almost knocked over my glass. Now I knew how to get Jeralynn and Etta Mae to like me. And if they liked me, maybe they'd like Poppy, too. "Mr. Bailey, can we practice bike riding again tomorrow?"

"Tomorrow evenin', if it ain't still rainin' and ain't too dark. You in a hurry all of a sudden?"

"No," I lied. "But you said that today is better than tomorrow. You make being a good rider sound like a lot of fun."

"It is. Maybe I'll get off work a little early, so we can practice before dark. That be all right?"

"Yes."

"If all your homework is done," Mama reminded me.

"It will be," I promised.

I'd see to it. Now there was a reason to learn, and quickly, too.

After supper, Mama invited Bailey to sit awhile, so he brought a rocker from the porch and put it by the fireplace. Mama did the dishes, and I sat at the table and did my homework. When I looked up, Bailey was gazing at my daddy's picture sitting on the dresser, next to the clock that I got to wind up every morning. That picture was one of Mama's treasures, the only photograph we owned. I'd sometimes find Mama holding it, looking into Daddy's smiling face. She'd put the picture down and turn away, muttering under her breath. I'd learned to keep quiet when she did that, because if I asked her what was wrong, she'd snap at me to let her be.

"This your daddy?" Bailey asked.

"Yes, sir."

"He was a handsome man. You must be proud of him, missuz."

Mama went on wiping a pot. "He was a hero," she said. "Died trying to save someone."

She didn't sound like she was proud, though. As usual, when the subject of Daddy came up, Mama sounded upset, almost angry.

"That so? What happened?"

"I don't like to talk about it."

"I see," Bailey replied, easing into the rocker. "Y'all must miss him."

"We do," Mama replied. "But missing someone doesn't bring him back."

"You remember your daddy?" he asked me.

"No, sir. He died when I was two years old."

"I knew my daddy a lot longer than that," Bailey said. "Glad I did. Sho' do miss him, though, even after all these years."

"What kind of man was he?" Mama asked. She had finished drying the pans and came to the table where I was working.

"He was the hardest workin' man I ever knowed. Could plow from before sunup till after sundown and then get up and do it again the next day, and the next. Could pick more cotton than any man I ever seen, saw more timber, build more fence. Never complained, neither. I never heard him say one evil word about any man, black or white."

"Hmmph," Mama snorted.

"Funny, the things we remember from years ago," Bailey said. "They's lots I can't recall about Daddy and the things he did, but some other things I can still see in my mind like they was yesterday. For instance, I'll never forget the first time I saw my daddy's naked back."

I wondered why Bailey remembered his daddy's back so well, and why he was telling us about it now.

Bailey didn't wait for Mama or me to say anything. "Guess I was five or so," he continued. "As usual, Daddy had worked hard in the field all day. I watched him unhitch his overalls, drop 'em to his waist, unbutton his blue work shirt, and peel it off his body. That shirt was wet through with his sweat. He turned from me to wash up in the bucket o' water Mama had pumped for him. That's when I saw the scars."

"Scars?" I asked. "What kind of scars? How did he get them?"

"Hush!" Mama exclaimed. "Mr. Bailey, don't you go telling Carissa all that mess."

I had to know. "How'd he get scars?" I repeated.

Bailey looked right at me. "Slave master's lash. From the times somebody thought he wasn't workin' hard enough or long enough, I reckon." He shook his head. "I can't imagine my daddy not workin' hard enough. Nor causin' no trouble, neither. There was no reason on earth anyone should want to whip that man."

I felt like crying. If someone could whip a man as good as Bailey's father, then someone could have whipped Bailey, too. Had he been whipped when he was a slave, even though he was just a little boy when slavery ended?

"And you claim that white folks aren't that bad!" Mama sounded very angry. "From what I've heard, a white man could *always* find a reason to whip a black man. Doesn't it make your blood boil when you think about what they did?"

"It used to. Made me crazy. They was lots of things in my life used to make me so angry at the world and people that sometimes it made me sick. But then one day I realized that holdin' on to them bad feelings— hatred, bitterness—was like holdin' a glowin' coal in my hand."

"What do you mean?" I asked. The thought of touching the red-hot embers in the fireplace made me feel shaky.

"Think about it. How long could you hold on to a live coal 'fore it'd burn you bad?"

"No time at all."

"That's right. You could pick up a coal, but jus' as soon as your fingers touched it, it would start doin' its work. You could try tellin' yourself that it wasn't burnin' you, and maybe if you used all your strength, you could manage to keep it in your hand for a second or two, but by that time the damage would be done. Coal burn right through you. I reckon stayin' mad at the world does jus' the same thing. Eat you right up if you let it. A long time ago, I decided to try an' let go of all that stuff. But, Lord, the temptation to pick it up again can sho' be strong. Sometimes even now I grasp onto that ol' anger and hatred. Know what happens then?"

I thought I knew. "They still burn?"

"They still burn. Jus' like they always did. I wasn't there when my daddy died. I told you I left home when I was in my twenties. When I went back, ten years later, Mama was livin', but Daddy was gone. Dropped dead behind a mule doin' spring plowing, Mama said. She showed me where he was buried in Mt. Moriah churchyard. There warn't no marker, jus' some bottles sunk upside down in the ground around the grave. I'm sorry I warn't there with him when he died." Bailey stopped talking and stared at the floor.

"Get back to your homework now," Mama told me after a minute. I did. Mama and Bailey didn't say anything else, and in a little while, Bailey went to his shed.

✿

The next morning, Poppy was wearing one of her old dresses, faded and frayed at the hem but clean and pressed. She had on white socks and her new black shoes, which had been polished. I had on my new dress again—Mama had managed to dry it in front of the fireplace—and my shoes, which Mama had dried by stuffing them with soft rags and placing them on the hearth. She'd gotten up early to repolish them.

Mama gave me my dinner, and I put *Little Women* into my binder. The book's cover was still damp, and it was blotchy where the dye had run. I also had the note Mama had written to Miss Johnson about it.

Before we left, Mama lectured us. "I want you two to promise me you won't go messing with those girls today, or any day. If you run into them on the road and they start up with you, you turn around and come home. I'll walk you if I have to. And if they cause more trouble, I'll speak to Miss Johnson and to their folks. But if you start anything, Poppy, I won't lift a finger to help you, and neither will Carissa, because I told her not to."

Poppy looked so pitiful that I felt sorry for her, despite all the trouble she had caused me yesterday. Not only that, but I wondered what I *would* do if Jeralynn and Etta Mae attacked her again. Yesterday I hadn't planned on running to help, but I had anyway, before I could stop to think about it. Promising Mama was one thing. What I would actually do was another.

"Carissa got herself into enough trouble by putting her nose into your business," Mama went on. "I won't stand for another mess like that. Do you two understand me?"

We nodded that we did, and Mama sent us on our way.

Etta Mae and Jeralynn were in the playground waiting for Miss Johnson to open the door. Jeralynn smirked at us and whispered something to Etta Mae, but then they both ignored us. Maybe their parents had heard a version of the story—after all, both Jeralynn and Etta Mae had gotten home all muddy, too—and had told them to leave us alone. I hoped so.

I handed Miss Johnson Mama's note and showed her *Little Women*. She said she understood why I had done what I did, but she hoped Poppy and I had learned our lesson. And next time, she added, I shouldn't take a book out of doors if there was *any* chance of its getting wet. Books were too valuable to treat carelessly. I felt bad when she said that, but Miss Johnson said to go ahead and enjoy reading it. That helped. Now, if only I could keep Poppy from messing with those girls until I could put my plan into action, everything would be all right.

❧

That evening, and all that week, Bailey never got home from work until after dark, not even on Saturday, so I had to wait six days for my next bicycle lesson. Finally, after dinner on Sunday, he invited me to ride.

"What about Poppy?" I asked. "I can run down and get her."

"We'll let Miss Poppy be. This lesson is jus' for you. She can practice another time soon."

I climbed onto the bicycle, and Bailey told me how to brake. Then he gave me his usual advice: "Keep pedalin' hard, even after I let go. Hold on and aim straight ahead. Find your balance."

"Will I know when I do?"

"Sho' will. If you feel yourself start goin' over to one side, jus' lean the other way a little bit. If you go too far and start to fall, lean back the other way. It jus' take a little practice."

I pedaled and Bailey ran alongside, holding on to the back of the seat. He gradually loosened his grasp, and I began to wobble to the right. "Lean left!" he cried. I did—and almost fell over that way. "Not too much," he advised. So I came back to the middle. Suddenly, I understood. *I* was in control of the bike. If it started to tilt, I could right it. Balance wasn't something out there for me to find, like in a game of hide-and-seek. It was something inside myself.

"You're doin' fine," Bailey said. "Keep goin'." He relaxed his hold on the seat, and I wobbled again but found my balance more quickly this time.

We got to the crossroads, and I braked. "How did that feel?" he panted.

"I'm finding it!"

"'Course you are. Let me get my wind back and we'll try again."

The next time down the road, Bailey held so lightly that I couldn't even tell, unless I began to wobble. Then his strong hand steadied the bike and gave me confidence. When we stopped the second time, I was ready to try it on my own.

"Get me started and then let go," I told him.

"You sure?"

"I know I can do it."

We got going, and then Bailey gave me an extra push and released me. For a second, I was afraid I'd crash. I began to tilt to the right, so I leaned to the left and came back upright. I was doing it! I had found my balance!

"Keep going!" I heard Bailey shout far behind me. Down, down the road I pedaled as the cool October air rushed against my face. How I wished Mama could see me, and Etta Mae and Jeralynn, too. They didn't know how to ride a bicycle—but I did.

Finally, I came to a stop in front of Poppy's. I left the bicycle in the road, ran to her door, and knocked, but there was no answer. Disappointed, I went back to the bicycle. Could I get started on my own? I got back on, moved the pedals so that the right one was all the way at the top, and pushed down hard with my right foot. Then I got my left foot onto the left pedal. "Keep going," I ordered myself. "Find your balance." As I moved forward, my balance came to me. Straight up the road I went, Bailey growing larger every second. Then there was Mama, standing on the porch, beaming at me. "Hey, Mama! Hey, Mr. Bailey!" I shouted, zooming past, a silver and blue arrow, racing through the air toward my target. No— I was the *Pegasus,* cutting through majestic combers.

I rode past our house and continued on toward Etta Mae's. Maybe she would be sitting on her porch and see me whiz by. But no one was there. Then I was passing Jeralynn's, but it, too, was deserted. I was ready to go back, and I slowed down to turn around. I moved the handlebars to the right, and the bike responded. Harder, harder—then a fence came into view. Panicking, I pulled extra hard to the right. The bicycle leaned. I tried to correct it, but it was too late. The wheel skidded, the fence loomed up before me, and I smashed into it. I hit the ground, and the bicycle fell on top of me.

For a minute, I lay there waiting for the pain to start. Certainly, I had a broken arm or leg. . . . But there was no pain. I seemed to be perfectly all right. It was good to know that I could fall off a bicycle and not get hurt.

The sound of running footsteps came up behind me, and then Bailey and Mama pulled the bicycle off of me and turned me over. "You all right, Carissa?" Mama asked, brushing dirt out of my face.

"Yes. I was trying to turn and come back to you. I did it, didn't I?"

"You done fine," Bailey said, beaming at me. I pulled myself to my feet, brushed myself off, and started to reach for the bicycle. "That's my girl." He stood the bicycle up. I got on, shook off his offer to help me get started, and wobbled off. "The turns are tricky," he called after me. "Give yourself plenty o' room." I decided not to try any more turns but eased to a stop right in front of our house.

I had found my balance. Now I could ride, and I could finish making my plan.

EIGHT

Later that afternoon, Bailey invited me to go for a walk. I asked if Poppy could come, too, and he said yes. So I raced down to her house to see if she was home yet. She was, and Miss Dolores said she could come. We ran back to our place, and soon the three of us were headed toward the country. Poppy talked without stopping and ran and skipped back and forth so much that it seemed she was taking twice as many steps as Bailey and I were.

Bailey kept a slow and steady pace, just like the tortoise in the story. He pointed out lots of things—how there were different kinds of goldenrod in bloom, how a hawk could soar without even having to flap his wings, and how a fence lizard blended so well with the bark of the scrub oaks that we could hardly see him, even close up. Soon Poppy had her pockets stuffed with things Bailey had shown us: a prickly sweetgum ball; a snake skin; a broken piece of Indian pottery; the flat, dried body of a dead bat.

Poppy liked the bat the best. "You can still feel his fur," she said, stroking its front and holding the creature out to me. "Touch it."

Bats got into our cabin once in a while and frightened Mama half to death; she said they'd fly at your head and get tangled in your hair. But this tiny thing didn't look dangerous. In my palm, it weighed next to nothing. I could make out its two small ears, and a little mouth with the smallest teeth I'd ever seen. Poppy was right: its chest did still have a patch of fur on it, soft to the touch.

"Look at this," Bailey called, as Poppy and I inspected the bat's body. He came up to us and held out a small wad of hair and bones.

"What is it?" I asked.

"Owl pellet."

"What's that?" Poppy asked.

"His droppings," Bailey said.

Poppy looked at him blankly.

"His poo-poo."

"Ick!" she exclaimed, pulling back her hand.

"You can see what he eats for breakfast," Bailey

went on. "Lot o' mice and moles and stuff. Digests the good meat, and the rest, like hairs and bones"—Bailey poked his finger into the pellet, which broke apart at his touch—"the rest goes right on through."

Poppy wouldn't put the pieces of the pellet into her pocket, and I figured there was some hope for her, after all.

We were well into the country now, with fields of picked-over cotton on either side of us. "You ever picked cotton?" Bailey asked me.

"No. Mama says she'd rather starve than pick cotton or let me do it. People used to ask us, but Mama always said no."

"Can't say I blame her, providin' she can make it by doin' laundry and such. Pickin' cotton is some hard work."

"Mr. Bailey, you said your daddy could pick a lot of cotton. Did you have to pick it, too, when you were a slave?" I was still wondering if Bailey had ever been whipped, but I was afraid to ask about that. Maybe he'd tell me on his own if I got him to talking about slavery days.

"No, honey, I picked cotton later, when my family sharecropped. I was only a little fellow when the slaves were freed. . . . Seems like I remember the day we found out, like maybe master came an' told us. Or might be I jus' heard so much about it in later years that my memory wants me to think I recall it myself. That must o' been a great day, though—the day we were free."

"What happened after that?"

"My mama and daddy took all us children and left where we'd been livin'. They finally found a place where a white man needed workers, and he offered Daddy a cabin and a mule if Daddy would farm for him. That's where we ended up stayin'—over in west Georgia, not all that far from where we started from. Free, but workin' on someone else's land."

"You didn't like that. You said you didn't."

"No, honey, I didn't. Freedom didn't feel free. So as soon as I could, I left. 'You're a free man, Bailey,' I kept tellin' myself. 'Don't save up freedom for some future day. Live it now.' Guess that's why I've been a wanderer all these years—never have used up all the freedom they is. Hope I never will."

I hadn't ever thought about being free, not in the way Bailey was talking about it. No one had ever owned me or made me do things I didn't want to do. But Mama and I didn't have our own land, and I knew Mama would rather do something besides the white folks' laundry. There were no other ways for her to make a living, though, so maybe we weren't free, after all. Not if freedom meant we could leave Summit whenever we wanted to. I thought of Mama and me on bicycles, traveling from place to place the way Bailey had, finding enough work to buy food, sleeping under the stars. The idea sounded good to me, but Mama would never be happy doing that. All she wanted was to get back north and live in a big city.

Bailey mopped his face with his handkerchief. "Mighty warm in the sunshine. How about we find us some shade and have a rest?"

Sand hills rose up on either side of the road, but we found a stand of puny oaks where the ground was level and sat in the dappled shade beneath the trees. Bailey took out his pipe and tobacco and began to smoke, while Poppy drew lines and circles in the soft sand with a sharp stick.

"You ever hear about the squirrel that tried to save up the daylight?" Bailey asked us between puffs.

"Is it a story?" Poppy asked. "I like stories."

"Yes. You girls want to hear it?"

We said yes.

"This story takes place a long time ago, way back at the beginnin' of the world. God made the world in the springtime, so the first thing the critters saw was the daylight gettin' longer and longer, and the nights shorter and shorter. 'Course, the owls and possums and 'coons didn't like that, 'cause night was when they found their food. And some of the lazy critters that liked to sleep all the time didn't like the idea, either.

"So spring turned into high summer, and the days got to their longest. Then they stopped gettin' longer and jus' stayed the same, and it seemed for a while that the good Lord had finished fiddlin' around with his creation and had found jus' the right balance. Most everybody seemed satisfied, 'specially the squirrels. One squirrel in particular, the first squirrel of all and father to the rest, was mighty pleased with the arrangement.

"Then things started changin'. The days got cooler, and the sun began to rise a little later and later each day, and set a little earlier, too."

"Like now," Poppy said. "Mama told me yesterday morning—"

"Don't interrupt," I told her. She made a face at me. "Go on, Mr. Bailey."

"Ol' Mr. Squirrel got to worryin'," he said. "Shorter the days got, the more he worried. Finally, he got so upset, he called a meetin' of all the forest critters.

"'Way things are goin,' he said, 'we'll soon be in the dark and cold all the time, and what we gon' do then?'

"The other critters laughed at him. 'Lord ain't gon' put us in the dark and leave us there,' they said. 'If the days shorten up for a while, they'll lengthen back again in due time.'"

"How they know that?" Poppy asked. "Who told them?"

"Maybe the same way the critters know things today. The way the birds know to make nests, and the spiders to weave webs."

"Then why didn't Mr. Squirrel know the days would get longer again, if the other animals did?"

"Let Mr. Bailey tell the story," I scolded. Poppy could never keep still. But she had asked a smart question. Miss Johnson told Poppy she could be a good student if only she would learn to pay attention for more than ten seconds.

"I reckon Mr. Squirrel warn't too bright," Bailey told Poppy. "You'll hear more proof o' that in a little bit. Anyway, he couldn't rest easy in his mind. While all the other critters got busy storin' up food for the winter, he began lookin' around for somethin' to put light in so he could save it and bring it out when the world was in darkness. He saw one of his children playin' with a hickory nut and realized he had the solution to his problem. He would gather the warm daylight in the nuts and store 'em up for when the sun went out and it was gon' be dark and cold all the time."

"You can do that?" Poppy asked.

"Of course not," I said.

"You ever try it?" Bailey asked me.

"No! Don't tease. Just tell the story." I was getting impatient with Poppy, and with that stupid squirrel, too.

Bailey said he was sorry for teasing me, and continued. "Them hickory nuts was already full of good, sweet nutmeats, and that left no room for the daylight. So Mr. Squirrel gathered up as many as he could, broke 'em in half real careful with his strong teeth, and then scraped out the innards. His family tried to tell him he was wastin' good food, but he wouldn't listen. Soon, he had hundreds of hickory nuts broke in half, layin' in the sunshine. They was all jus' as full of warm daylight as they could be.

"How was he gon' keep that golden light inside

while he was hidin' the nuts for later? He reckoned he had to hide 'em, considerin' how all the other critters would come around lookin' for warmth and light in the black darkness.

"He put the top back on each nut, and they fit together okay, but the tops wouldn't stick to the bottoms. Mr. Squirrel sat and thought 'bout it, till finally he got an idea. He ran to the bee tree and asked the Queen if he could have some beeswax. She had her workers push a big lump out of the hive. He grabbed that wax in his teeth and ran back to his nuts. He spent days puttin' the two halves of each nut together and sealin' 'em shut with that sticky beeswax."

"My mama melted wax and poured it on jars of peach jam to preserve it," Poppy said.

"So what?" I cried. "Stop talking!"

"You stop," Poppy shot back. "You always tellin' me what to do."

"Somebody has to."

"The story's almost done, if you ladies care to hear the rest of it," Bailey broke in.

"I do," I said. "Poppy's the one interrupting."

Poppy started to say something, but Bailey put his finger to her lips. "You jus' interested, that's all," he told her. "Let me tell you how it turned out."

He puffed on his pipe a moment before he went on. "In the early mornings, while all the other critters was still in they beds, Mr. Squirrel went and buried all them nuts in a secret place. Then he felt right satisfied, knowin' that when the world fell into freezin' darkness, he could go dig up a nut, open it, and have a little bit o' summertime all to himself.

"Well, it turned into fall and then into winter. When the food began to get scarce, the other squirrels started feastin' on the pinecones and nuts they had stored up, but Ol' Mr. Squirrel didn't have many for himself, 'cause he'd spent so much time savin' daylight. He got hungrier and hungrier, but he reckoned that when the full darkness come along, he'd be the one warm and laughin' while everyone else was cryin' in the dark.

"Finally, it got to the darkest day of the year. 'I can't wait no longer,' thought Mr. Squirrel. 'I'm hungry, but I don't have to sit here in the dark and cold as well. I'll jus' open me some of my hickory nuts and get me some light and heat.' So he went and dug up three nuts. He went to open the first nut. It was sealed tight with that beeswax, but he finally broke it with a stone. But instead of it bein' full of light and heat—"

"There was nothin'," Poppy declared.

"How'd you know?" Bailey asked. "I thought you said you'd never heard this story."

"It not hard to figure out. Mr. Squirrel was some stupid."

"Dumb as a post," Bailey agreed. "He tried the next one, figurin' the first one might o' had a leak he couldn't see. Same story. Nothin'. Tried the third one—same thing. 'It's not fair!' he cried. 'All my hard work wasted.'

"Then he heard someone laughin'. He turned round

and there was his head wife. 'What's so funny?' he asked.

"'You are. Did you really think we got to save up the sunshine? Is the One who gave us light and warmth gon' take 'em away again? Maybe they's gon' be times when it's more dark than light, but the light is always gon' be there for us. We don't have to try an' save it for tomorrow. Better to enjoy it today.'

"Mr. Squirrel felt mighty foolish, but he knew in his heart that his wife was right.

"'I reckon you's hungry,' she told him. 'Come on now and get some food.'

"So he did. And from that day on, Ol' Mr. Squirrel never tried to save no daylight in hickory nuts. But his children and grandchildren found out about what he done, and to this day, sometimes you'll see one of 'em diggin' up a nut and breakin' it open, jus' to see for themselves if maybe he was right."

"I like that story," Poppy said. "You told it good, Mr. Bailey."

"Thank you," he said. "How about you, Carissa? You like it?"

I thought the story was silly, something for little children. But if I said so, Poppy would get all mad. She'd think I was calling her a baby for liking it. Besides, I didn't want to hurt Bailey's feelings.

"It was good," I said. "Thank you for telling it."

"You welcome," Bailey said. "I might tell y'all another one sometime."

He leaned against a tree and looked around at the

sand hills rising up twenty feet from where we sat among the scrub oaks. "Do you ladies know why all these sand hills are here?"

"Why?" I asked back.

"Nobody told y'all—for real?"

I looked at Poppy, who just shook her head.

"No," I answered for both of us.

"Let me ask you a question. What is the beach made of?"

I let Poppy have such an easy question. "Sand," she answered.

"Right, at least down here. Up north, they got some rocky beaches. But here in the South, all sand. And what's this all round us?"

"Sand," she repeated.

"You a lot smarter than Mr. Squirrel!" he said. "So how are the two connected?"

Poppy shrugged. "Don't know," she said.

I had an answer, but it seemed too crazy to be possible. If I was wrong, Poppy would laugh at me. But if I was right, Bailey would see which one of us was smarter. "The ocean was here once?" I said.

"That's right."

Pleased to be correct, I gave Poppy a superior look.

"Naw!" Poppy cried. "You playin', Mr. Bailey! Ocean's miles and miles away from here."

"How would you know?" I asked. "You've never been there."

"You, neither."

"'Bout eighty miles away," Bailey said. "But it warn't always so. Once—long time ago—millions and zillions of years ago, I hear—the ocean was right here."

"When God sent the flood?" I asked.

"You mean in ol' Noah's time? Maybe. Let's say it was. So what happened when that flood came to an end?"

"The water went down."

"That's right. Ocean went back to its natural bed, where it is today. But that didn't happen in a day. Couldn't. Too much water for it to drain out all at once. Took time. So once upon a time, all them years ago, ocean was right nearby, and this big sand hill was part o' the beach."

"For real? You *are* playin'," Poppy said.

"For real."

"Then where are all the seashells?" I asked. If Bailey couldn't answer, I'd know he really was joking with us.

"All ground to bits," he said without stopping to think. "Shells break real easy. Step on 'em, they bust. Any shells that was here got ground down to powder long ago. Only sand left."

I looked around at the road, at the sand hills on either side of it, at the little oaks, and tried to imagine all of it under water. It didn't seem possible. Summit, Canoochee Road, our cabin . . .

As we headed home, Bailey was deep into his own thoughts. Poppy had run on ahead, chasing after a stray cat that had seen us coming and disappeared into a ditch. Bailey stopped and put his hand on my shoulder. "You got to promise me something," he said.

"What?"

"You promise me that one day you'll go see the ocean. You go, hear me? Feel the wind in your face, that sand between your toes, the taste of salt water in your mouth. You duck your head under and splash all around, make a fool out o' yo'self if you want to. Pick up lots o' seashells to bring home and put 'em on a shelf to remind yo'self that you been to the sea. You can go anywhere you want to, Carissa. We's free, understand? Don't let no one else decide what you can and can't do. If life in one place is squeezin' you too hard, get up and find you a better place. You get up and go when you're ready, you hear?"

Bailey had never talked to me so seriously before. It made me feel like a grownup. Poppy wouldn't understand, but I did—a little, at least. And I realized that the story of Mr. Squirrel might not be so silly after all. What had Bailey said about not saving up freedom, but using it when you had it?

"You listenin', Carissa?" Bailey said.

"Yes, sir."

"Promise me. You're gon' go to the ocean one day."

"I promise."

He smiled. "Good girl. And speakin' o' goin' places, we better get home. Don't want your mama worryin' about us." He looked down the road. "Now, where'd that Poppy get to? She's the slipperiest young'un I ever did see."

✺

"Mr. Bailey," I asked as we neared our cabin, "can I ride your bicycle to school sometime?" I'd been wanting to ask him this for a while, but I didn't think he would trust me with his most valuable possession. From the way he'd just talked to me about freedom, though, I knew he didn't think I was a child anymore. Maybe he would let me take it.

Riding the bicycle to school was the most important part of my plan to get Jeralynn and Etta Mae to like me. No one else had a bike, and if I could ride to school, the other children would be interested. They would want to touch the bike and ask me about it. I could explain how I'd learned to ride. I could tell them about Bailey and all the things he'd done. Then Jeralynn and Etta Mae would see I was popular, and they'd want to be friends.

"I don't see why not," Bailey said right away. "Once you get a chance to practice some more, and if I don't have to work one day, I reckon you can. How about I come along, too, and we show the children how to ride?"

This was even better than my plan. "Could we really?" I cried.

"'Course we could. But you gotta ask your teacher if it's okay."

I asked Miss Johnson the next day, and she said

yes. So I practiced every chance I got. Poppy learned, too, with just one more lesson from Bailey. In two weeks, we were both good riders. Turns were no problem; we could make a circle, reverse direction, and go the other way. Figure eights were easy. Poppy even learned to ride without holding onto the bars.

But now we had a problem. Every time Bailey let us use his bicycle, we both wanted to ride it. That meant we had to take turns, and it was no fun sitting on the porch watching the other person ride.

One Sunday not long afterward, I returned to our yard after my ride and found Poppy pouting. "You take too long," she complained. "I been waitin' a hour for you to get back. It ain't fair."

"I was only gone ten minutes." I didn't really know how long it had been, but ten minutes didn't sound like enough for Poppy to complain about.

"You were not. You said you were gon' be gone only a few minutes and it been a hour."

"Come on and take your turn, and stop telling lies. I wasn't gone that long and you know it."

She grabbed the bicycle. "I'm gon' stay gone jus' as long as you," she announced.

Poppy *was* gone a long time—much longer, I was sure, than I had been. By the time she breezed back into our yard, I was plenty angry. "If you ever take Mr. Bailey's bike for so long again, I won't let you use it," I snapped.

"Ain't yours to let. It belong to him, not you."

"Get off," I told her. "It's my turn."

"Have it." But instead of waiting for me to take it from her, Poppy let the bicycle fall over on its side.

"I'm telling Mr. Bailey!" I shouted. "He won't let you ever ride his bicycle again! You don't know how to take care of anything."

"I don't care. I'm gon' get me a bike of my own."

"You are not. Your mama can't afford it."

"Can, too. You'll see."

And with that, she marched down the road like someone with something to prove.

Next morning, Poppy showed up to walk with me to school, just as usual. She didn't mention our quarrel, and neither did I. Mama had said it wasn't worth staying mad about; besides, Poppy was my best friend. Almost my only friend.

I was doing homework that afternoon, just before it got dark, when Poppy burst into our cabin. "C'mon and see what I got," she crowed, beckoning Mama and me toward the yard. By the time we followed her out, there she was, standing proudly beside a bicycle that looked to be just about her size.

"Whose is that?" I asked, hurrying down the steps. "You didn't steal it, did you?"

"You tell the truth, now, girl," Mama added. "If you took that bike, you get it back to its owner before the sheriff comes and takes you away."

"I did not steal it! Mama got it for me today. It's my birthday present."

"It's not your birthday," I said. "Your birthday is in February."

"Mama say it an early present."

The bicycle wasn't new—that was for sure. Its frame had once been red, probably, but now the color was dulled to a muddy brown, a lot like the clay road. The metal trim was scratched, and the front fender looked as if it had been badly dented and then hammered back into shape.

As I looked at the bicycle, a terrible, sick feeling rose up inside me. I didn't care about its nasty color, or how it wasn't shiny and new, or how the fender looked crumpled. All I cared about was one thing: Poppy had a bicycle of her own, and I didn't.

Mama came down the steps and stood by us in the road. "How'd your mama afford a bicycle?"

"She say a gentleman friend where she work got it for her."

I couldn't take my eyes off of the bicycle. How could it belong to her and not to me? I wanted to slap Poppy, grab the bicycle, and ride far away where no one could find me.

"Ride it, Carissa," she offered. "I told Mama I was gon' let you ride it first thing, since you and Mr. Bailey been so nice to me."

Poppy's generosity made me feel worse. I wondered if I'd be so ready to share a new bike.

"You're right sweet to offer that," Mama told her. "Go on, Carissa. Try it out."

I didn't want to, but how could I say no? "All right, if you want me to."

I got onto the bicycle.

"Tell Poppy thank you," Mama said.

"Thank you," I said, not even looking at Poppy.

"Go on," she urged. "Take a ride."

Right away I knew that the bicycle was too small for me. My legs were cramped, and it felt like my knees were going up to my shoulders.

I rode it for a few feet and came back. "It's nice," I forced myself to say, "but it's too small."

"We can raise the seat," Poppy suggested.

"That's all right," I said. "I don't think raising it will help. It's just too small."

"Jus' right for me!" Poppy cried, swinging onto it and launching herself. "Watch!" She darted down the road. I felt so jealous I wanted to cry.

Mama put her hand on my back and patted me the way she used to do when I was little and had hurt myself. "Look at that child go," she said. "Canoochee Road won't be safe for people now—not with her tearing up and down like hell on wheels."

"Mama!" I exclaimed, shocked. She never used bad words in front of me.

She laughed. "Well, it's true. She's going to kill someone or kill herself before she's done."

Poppy whizzed by us, took a sharp turn, and zoomed back, screeching to a halt within two feet of where we stood.

"That's a mighty fine bicycle, Miss Poppy," Mama told her. "I just hope you'll be careful and not knock somebody down."

"I won't. Is Mr. Bailey home? I want Carissa to ride with me."

"He's not home from work," I said sourly. "Besides, I have to do my homework. So do you," I added.

"It be fun to ride together," Poppy said.

I didn't say anything.

"Of course it will," Mama answered for me. "Lots of fun. But Carissa has to finish her homework now, and you better be getting home to yours, too. Besides, it'll be dark soon."

"Yes, ma'am. See you tomorrow," Poppy told me.

"I guess you're going to ride to school from now on," I said tightly. "You don't have to stop here for me."

"Mama say I can't ride to school. She afraid someone steal it. She say that all the boys and girls be jealous of me, now that I got a bicycle and they don't. So I still got to walk. See you!" she cried, and holding on with one hand and waving the other over her shoulder, she rode away.

I watched her disappear down the road. I almost wished she *would* crash into someone—preferably Jeralynn.

"Penny for your thoughts," Mama said.

I was afraid to say what I was thinking. It was ungrateful to be jealous of Poppy's good fortune. After all,

God had taken good care of Mama and me. He had sent Bailey to us. We had never gone without. Mama sometimes reminded me of how blessed we were, even though times were tough.

None of that mattered.

I knew I shouldn't tell, but I did anyway. "I want a bicycle, too. A new red one, all for myself. I want it more than anything."

I thought Mama would be angry, but she spoke gently. "I know, sugar. I wish with all my heart I could run out and buy you one right this minute. You'll never know how much I wish that."

I put my arm around Mama's waist, and without saying anything more, we went into the cabin to get supper.

NINE

❧

A while later, Mr. Satterwhite's aunt died. Since the hardware store would be closed for the funeral, Bailey wouldn't have to go to work that day. I told Miss Johnson that he could come and show the students how to ride, so in two days I pedaled proudly to school, with Poppy and Bailey walking alongside of me.

Miss Johnson introduced Bailey to the students. He sat in the back of the room for a while, then went outside and chopped wood for the stove while we did our lessons.

I had explained my plan to Poppy the day before.

"Everyone at school will be interested in the bicycle," I told her. "We can both show them how to ride, and then Bailey will teach them. Especially Jeralynn and Etta Mae. Then they'll like us for sharing Bailey and the bicycle. They won't give us any more trouble."

"Who cares about them?" Poppy complained. "They both nasty."

"They can change. And wouldn't you rather have them as friends than enemies? They're popular. If they like us, we'll have more friends, too."

"I don't care 'bout havin' more friends, not if I got to be nice to you-know-who. I hate 'em."

"Don't be so mean. We have to learn to get along. Mama says so."

"Then your mama can be they friends, not me."

"I'm going to try it," I persisted.

"I'll push 'em over when they ridin'," Poppy promised.

"No, you won't! If you can't help, then you'd better not do anything to mess things up."

Poppy could be stubborn, but I made her promise not to cause trouble. My plan just needed a chance.

"Carissa's friend Mr. Bailey was nice enough to bring his bicycle today," Miss Johnson said before dismissing us for dinner and recess. "You children have been working extra hard lately, and as a reward, you will not have any afternoon lessons. Mr. Bailey has generously offered to show all of you how to ride a bicycle, if you wish to try."

After we had eaten, everyone crowded around the bicycle. Miss Johnson came out, too. Bailey had polished the bike extra well the night before, and it looked brand-new. "Now, y'all make a big circle," he said. "First, I'm gon' have Carissa ride a bit to show y'all how it's done."

I could have hugged him for that! I threw a leg over the bike, pushed off neatly, and began riding inside the circle of my schoolmates. Then Poppy insisted she have a turn, too, so Bailey let her.

"Who wants to try first?" Bailey asked, after Poppy had stopped.

Etta Mae pushed Jeralynn forward. "Naw, girl," Jeralynn protested. She giggled, put her hands over her face, and tried to turn back.

This fit my plan perfectly. I had wanted them to get first chance, and here was Etta Mae helping me out. She just didn't know it.

"Come on," Bailey urged. "You can do it."

Etta Mae shoved Jeralynn toward Bailey, who came in her direction. "Ain't nothin' to it," he promised. "'Sides, I won't let you fall."

"Go on," some of the children shouted.

"You scared, girl," others cried.

"I am not!"

"Prove it!" they shouted back.

"Okay, I will."

She strode up to the bicycle and put a leg over while Bailey held it from the other side.

I leaned over to Etta Mae. "I know she can do it," I whispered. "You can go next."

Etta Mae didn't even look at me.

"Now put your feet on the pedals," Bailey was instructing Jeralynn. Jeralynn was holding on to the handlebars as if they were a lifeline. The minute she put her other foot on the pedal, the bike started to tilt, and she let out a little scream. Bailey was holding the bike, though, and she didn't fall.

"She's just nervous," I assured Etta Mae. "She'll get it."

"Will or won't," Etta Mae said without interest.

"Now start pedalin'," Bailey told Jeralynn. The bike began to move. Jeralynn screamed—loud this time—let go of the handlebars, and grabbed her head. The children laughed and shouted. Jeralynn was big, a lot larger than I, and this time Bailey couldn't stop the bicycle from falling over. She had enough sense to jump clear, however, and somehow landed on her feet. The class cheered.

Jeralynn, her dignity in pieces, smoothed down her dress and stalked off.

"Who's next?" Bailey asked.

No one volunteered.

"You go," I whispered to Etta Mae. "I know you can do it. Then everyone will try."

"If *you* can ride, reckon I can jus' as good. . . . Let me," she told Bailey. She didn't ask—she told.

Bailey helped her on and told her what to do, and

she began to pedal. "Let go!" she shouted to Bailey. "I can git it." She wobbled a couple of times, and once it looked as though she was going to fall, but to my astonishment, on and on she went, down the little path that led from the school to the road. We saw her reach the road, turn toward the right, and disappear.

Two of the smaller boys ran after her. When they got to the road, they called, "Look at 'er go! She gon' go all de way to Garfield, sure!"

I felt betrayed. "She already knew how to ride," I said loudly. "She already knew."

"Sho' look like it," Bailey agreed.

"It's not fair," I said.

"How so?"

"She should have told me the truth."

"Holdin' out on you, eh?"

I didn't appreciate the twinkle in his eye.

In a minute, Etta Mae came back, screaming, "How do I stop?"

"Back-pedal!" Bailey yelled.

It was too late. Etta Mae headed right for the crowd of children gathered to watch her approach. She turned to the left—too sharply—and the bicycle fell over.

"Look like she's a beginner, after all," Bailey whispered to me.

"Then how could she ride without falling?" I asked.

Etta Mae picked herself up. "That was fun," she exclaimed. "Can I go again?"

"You already knew how to ride," I declared.

"Did not. I never been on no bicycle before in my life."

"Some folks jus' got the natural talent for it," Bailey said. "You sho' is one of 'em."

Now I felt even angrier. It wasn't fair that someone like Etta Mae could figure out how to balance the first time, when it had been so hard for me. And why did Bailey have to pay her a compliment?

"Thank you," she replied primly. "Can I go again?"

"If they's time. Maybe some of the others want to try."

They did. As a flood of my schoolmates clamored for a turn, Etta Mae headed into the schoolhouse. I followed, and Poppy trotted after me. There was Jeralynn, pouting.

I was feeling annoyed with Etta Mae, but I still wanted my plan to work. "Please try again," I told Jeralynn. "You should have seen Etta Mae. It's not too hard. You can do it."

"It's easy," Etta Mae agreed.

A warm feeling surged up in my chest. Etta Mae was taking my side.

Jeralynn got to her feet. "All right. You two can do it, so can I."

"When you learn, we can all take turns riding," I announced. "Poppy, too. Her mama got her a bicycle. I know Mr. Bailey will let us use his whenever we want."

Jeralynn seemed not to have heard me. She walked

past us and went out the door. The rest of us followed behind.

Little Caleb Williams was on the bicycle now, looking as scared as a rabbit in a trap. Bailey was running alongside, panting. Caleb finally got the hang of it, a bit, and then Essie wanted her turn. Then Bailey had to have a rest, and more children tried, but finally Jeralynn was next.

This time she did better. She pedaled, Bailey held on, and after about three tries, she went a short way on her own. Bailey had told her how to brake, and she managed that well enough that she stopped the bicycle without falling. Without so much as a thank you to Bailey, she walked away.

I ran after her. "I knew you could do it! Now we can all ride together."

Jeralynn stopped and faced me. "You crazy, girl," she said. "I don't care nothin' 'bout you or that ol' bicycle. Who do you think you is?"

She might as well have punched me in the stomach. "You wanted to ride! You, too," I told Etta Mae. "Mr. Bailey said you have natural talent. He's right! We can be friends," I said desperately. "Poppy, too. We can do lots of things together."

"You wrong there," Jeralynn said.

"I never did anything to you. Why don't you like me?"

"Do I gotta have a reason? Jus' don't."

I wanted to disappear.

"Come on," Jeralynn said to Etta Mae. "I'm gett
me a drink o' water."

They strode away together.

"I told you it wouldn't work," Poppy said. "T
always been mean, and they always gon' *stay* mea

My face burned with embarrassment. I loo
around to see if anyone was watching. Where cou
run? Nowhere. But I wasn't going to let anyone se
cry, not even Poppy. "Come on," I told her. I wipe
face with my skirt, and we joined the others.

For another hour, I stood in the ring of childre
watched Bailey trying to teach them to ride. Some
aged it pretty well; some were too terrified to do
than clutch onto the handlebars while Bailey w
them around. Miss Johnson got on the bike and
for a short ride, too. She told us she'd learned
she was a child. Everyone had a good time, esp
Etta Mae and Jeralynn, who joined in the chee
jeers as if they had not just put a knife into m
and twisted it for fun.

When everyone who was big enough had
chance, Miss Johnson thanked Bailey. He
wanted to talk to her for a minute and asked me
for him. Poppy and I stood guarding the bicycl
of the children thanked me, but Etta Mae and
walked past us as if we were invisible.

I was struggling against tears when Baile
came out of the building. "I was tellin' Miz
that the county should fix up this place some,'

"It sho' does need it." He shook his head. "It's jus' a low-down dirty shame the way you children are treated. This building ain't hardly fit for hogs, let alone young'uns."

Then he looked at me closely. "What's the matter, Carissa?"

I couldn't speak.

"What's wrong, sugar?" He turned to Poppy. "How 'bout you ride my bicycle home? You can wait there for Carissa and me. Tell Miz Lorena we'll be along in a little."

Poppy beamed. Bailey lowered the seat for her; then she hopped onto the bicycle and rode away.

"Now, what's the problem? You look like you jus' lost your last friend."

"I thought—I thought Jeralynn and Etta Mae would like me if I brought the bicycle and let them ride."

"You thought you could buy their friendship?" Bailey asked.

His words shocked me. "No! Nothing like that."

"Like what, then?" He looked at me frowning, not unkindly, but as if he really wanted me to help him figure it out.

"I—I don't know."

"Sounds like boughten friendship to me."

It hurt me that Bailey would say that again.

"I wasn't buying anything!"

"Maybe not with money, but with offerin' to do somethin' nice for 'em. Ain't that kind o' the same thing?"

I was starting to understand, but I felt ashamed to admit why I had done it. Besides, Bailey might be disappointed in me. "I thought we were supposed to do nice things for other people. The preacher says so."

"'Course we are. But did you want them girls to learn to ride so *they* could have fun, enjoy themselves, or so they would like *you?*"

Bailey was right. I didn't care if Jeralynn was having a good time. I never wondered if Etta Mae was having fun.

"So they would like me," I admitted. "You said your bike made people want to talk to you. I thought if I could ride it to school, people would want to be my friend."

"I see," Bailey said. "But it's more than havin' a bike. You got to act friendly yourself. Talk to people. Act interested in 'em."

"I tried!" I wailed. "They still don't like me. Why won't they?"

"I don't know. But that's their problem. You can't *make* nobody like you, and the sooner you learn that lesson, the better off you're gon' be."

"It isn't fair. I tried to be nice."

"Do you really like either o' them girls? Be honest."

"No."

"But you wanted them for friends anyway?"

"Only because they're popular. If they liked me, I thought the other children would, too."

"I see."

I looked at the ground. "I'm stupid," I said. "It was a dumb plan."

Bailey patted my shoulder. "Now, don't you go sayin' that 'bout yourself. You ain't stupid. Maybe jus' a little lonely for some girls yo' own age. Don't you go mopin' now. You made a mistake, that's all. Nobody can blame you for that. Poppy's your good friend already, but sometimes it seems she's more your little sister than your friend."

I nodded.

"One day, you're gon' have a lot more friends," Bailey assured me.

"Really?"

"Yes, ma'am. You'll see. And one day you're gon' meet that one special man who's gon' make you his wife."

I couldn't help smiling at that.

"You ready to go home now?"

I was.

TEN

Once the pecans were in, Bailey started hinting about how good a pecan pie would taste, but Mama told him she didn't have any corn syrup. The next day, he brought home two bottles, plus several cups of pecan meats that he'd picked out of the shell. Mama said that he really must be hungry for a pie, and she agreed to bake him one soon.

So one Saturday in early November, after Bailey went to work, Granma came over and made the crusts while Mama mixed up the filling. She added chopped nuts, mixed again, and poured the filling into the crusts. Granma used whole pecan halves to decorate the tops, and Mama put the pies in the oven. They came out brown and crackly. I was ready for a big piece right away, but Mama said they were a special treat for Bailey, after all he'd done for us, and I'd have to wait until he got home at suppertime.

But Bailey didn't come home. Mama kept his supper warm until the clock said it was almost nine; then she finally let me have some pie while she cleaned up the kitchen, grumbling about "men who think women have nothing better to do than stand by the stove ready to feed them." He still hadn't returned when I went to bed. "Not home yet," Mama said when she came in later. "And it's past midnight. He's probably out somewhere drinking."

Now I was wide awake. "Does Mr. Bailey drink?"

"Probably. Most men do."

"I never saw him." I couldn't imagine Bailey drinking.

"That doesn't mean a thing except that he doesn't drink around *you*. He'd better not, either, if he wants to stay here."

"Did *you* ever see him drink?"

"No. I can't say I have. But some men can go for a long time—months . . . years, even—without touching a drop of whiskey, and then for some reason they go off half-crazy and get drunk and stay drunk for days. I pray to God that Bailey isn't one of them."

"I hope nothing happened to him."

"I hope not, too, sugar. He's probably just off having a good time with some of the men he knows in Summit. Lord knows he's earned a good time for himself once in a while, as hard as he works. I'm sure he's okay. Now, go to sleep."

Mama didn't sound convinced. It took me a long time to fall asleep, and I could tell that she was lying beside me, awake and wondering, just as I was.

Bailey didn't show up until dark the next day. By that time, Mama was worried, and so was Granma. She had come home with us from church, as she often did on Sundays. She and Mama had made a good dinner, and a lot of pecan pie was waiting to be eaten. That afternoon, they sorted laundry and did some mending, and Poppy came up with her bicycle, expecting that I'd be able to borrow Bailey's and go riding. Instead, we looked at books under the magnolia tree, but the afternoon grew chilly and we went inside, where it was warmer.

Just as Mama was putting out some leftovers for supper, Bailey appeared at the door. A silver stubble covered his cheeks and chin, and he looked tired. "'Evenin'," he said. "How is everyone? 'Evenin', Miz Rachel."

"Mr. Bailey," Granma said, not very friendly.

Mama put her hands on her hips and looked him straight in the eye. "We're about worried sick wondering where *you've* been—that's how we are. What were you thinking, going off to heaven knows where without saying a word to anyone? We've been sitting here praying that you hadn't fallen off that bicycle and broken your neck."

"Hi, Mr. Bailey," I said. "I'm glad you're not hurt."

Poppy said nothing, just went right up to him and hugged him. He patted her on the head.

"I'm sho' sorry, missuz. Charlie, the man I work with at Satterwhite's, he invited me to his place down toward Stillmore last night. He said he had some friends had a small hog they'd be cookin' all day and wanted me to help 'em eat it. Then he said we could go fishin' first thing this morning and fish all day if they was bitin'. I didn't have any way to let you know my plans, and—well, I reckon it jus' didn't occur to me to let y'all know. I'm mighty sorry if I worried you."

"So you were off eating and probably drinking, and then spent all the day with a fishing pole in your hand and never thought we might be fretting. I call that inconsiderate."

"He *is* a grown man, Lorena," Granma put in. "Since when do he have t' let anyone know his plans?"

"He forgot," Mama grumbled, loud enough that Bailey was bound to hear. "Come on, then, and have some supper. I guess your stomach didn't forget it's time to eat."

Then Bailey spotted the pie on the table. "Aw, missuz, you went and made me a pecan pie like I asked, and I wasn't here to get it. No wonder you's mad at me. You went to all that trouble, and I stood you up. I'm truly sorry."

"I accept your apology," she said, taking a pan of biscuits out of the oven. "Now, everybody come and eat—you, too, Poppy—while I warm up this pie."

I wanted to hear all about Bailey's weekend with his friends, but he didn't mention it, and I figured it was better not to ask. He kept on telling Mama how delicious her cooking was, and when the warm pie came out of the oven, he ate three pieces.

After supper, Bailey went with Poppy as she rode home. He said he didn't want her going alone in the dark.

"That Dolores Toliver must not care a thing about what her child does," Mama said as she began to work on my hair. Getting it combed and oiled on Sunday evenings had been part of my weekly routine for as long as I could remember. "If it got dark and *you* weren't home, you can bet I'd be walking up and down Canoochee Road, asking everyone if they'd seen you. As many tramps as there are wandering around on the roads, it isn't safe for a child to be out alone, especially at night."

We hadn't seen any tramps for a long time, not since Bailey came, so I wasn't sure why Mama would say that. It seemed that she always needed something to worry about.

"I wonder what that Bailey was really doing all weekend," she went on. "It just isn't like him to go off and not tell us."

"Ow!" I cried. It hurt where Mama was trying to pull the comb through my hair.

"I'm sorry, sugar," she said. "I don't know how your hair gets so tangled. . . . He could have ridden back here yesterday evening after work and told us he was going down to Stillmore. That wouldn't have taken long. Something just doesn't add up."

"Maybe he forgot, like he said."

"In all the months he's been around here, have you ever known that man to forget one thing?"

Mama was right, but I still believed Bailey. "He wouldn't lie to us."

"I don't like to think so, sugar. But you never know. You just never know."

❧

The Saturday before Thanksgiving, Mama went to Swainsboro. She had some extra money from pecans and wanted to shop for our Thanksgiving dinner. Bailey had arranged to have the day off, too, so all of us, including Granma, went along. Just as the sun was rising, we clambered into Deacon Braithwaite's wagon bed for the eleven-mile trip. Mama wrapped me in a quilt, and I nestled close against her and fell back to sleep as the wagon rolled noisily along the Swainsboro Road.

In town, we got a turkey from the poultry market. We had a crate to hold the turkey, and Bailey had promised to slaughter it the day before Thanksgiving. That left coffee, sugar, sweet potatoes, flour, onions, and several other things on Mama's list.

At Durden's general store, we went around to the

back door, where the colored customers entered. Then Mama had to wait for Mr. Durden to take care of all the white customers who came in one by one.

To pass the time, Mama looked over the piece goods, and Bailey examined the tools. Granma searched for a button to match one she'd lost from her Sunday dress. I peered into the glass case at the penny candy, clutching the nickel Bailey had given me to buy sweets. After I decided on some Mary Janes, peppermint sticks, and chewing gum, I walked to the front of the store and saw something that made me lose interest in everything else.

In the window was a girl's green bicycle. It looked just my size, too.

My dreams of a red bicycle burst like soap bubbles. I just *had* to have that green bicycle as my Christmas present. I approached it and ran my hand over the shiny green frame, imaging myself the envy of every child in Summit.

Then I glanced at the price tag: $38.95. Suddenly, I wanted to cry. Even though Bailey's help had made things easier for Mama, she could never, ever, afford a thirty-nine-dollar bicycle. If only—

Mama was still waiting for Mr. Durden's help, so I went over to get her. Bailey came, too. I took them up to the front window. "Look," I said.

"Oooh, what a lovely thing," Mama declared.

"Lot prettier than my ol' bike," Bailey agreed.

"Mama—"

She looked at me with understanding. "I know, sugar. Christmas."

I nodded.

She put her hand on my shoulder. "But you know that's impossible. Don't you?"

I nodded again. Mama pulled me close.

"Carissa is gon' have a bicycle all her own one day," Bailey asserted. "Mark my words."

"I hope so," Mama said.

"Lorena, I can help you now," Mr. Durden called.

Mama went to get her order filled. Bailey and I stayed by the bicycle.

"Don't you fret none 'bout it," Bailey told me. "I mean it when I say that one day you gon' have yourself a bike. Can't say when that day will be, but it's comin'."

I put my hand into Bailey's. We were still standing there when Mama said for me to come on and get my candy.

Going home that afternoon, I kept thinking about the green bicycle. Our turkey sat quietly in its crate, pecking at the dried corn Bailey had given it. When we got home, we'd put it in with our chickens, and it would live for a few more days, not suspecting a thing. "It's good you don't know what's comin'," Bailey told it. "Otherwise you wouldn't be so content."

I looked at the turkey and wished I were as brainless as it was. Why couldn't I be contented, too? If I weren't so greedy, I would be praying for the money Mama needed to buy train tickets back to

Philadelphia. But I couldn't help it. I didn't care about Philadelphia. I wanted that green bicycle.

I didn't watch when Bailey cut off the turkey's head on Wednesday night. He put the body in boiling water to loosen the feathers, and then plucked it and cleaned out its insides. When Mama set the golden brown turkey on the table the next day, I didn't think I would be able to eat any of it, but it smelled so good that my mouth began to water. I ended up eating a lot, with Mama's corn-bread-and-onion stuffing. I even said I wished we could have turkey more often, and Mama said that then it wouldn't be such a big treat.

On Saturday morning after Thanksgiving, Mama got ready to do some extra washing. Ladies in town had used their best linens over the holiday, so there were extra tablecloths, napkins, and tea towels to launder. Granma was coming to help, but it got on toward nine o'clock and she still had not arrived.

Finally, Mama got worried. "Carissa, run up to Granma's and make sure she's all right. It's not like her to oversleep, not with all this mess to take care of today." I pulled on my coat and walked the half-mile to Granma's cabin.

When I got to the porch, I could hear a strange noise coming from inside, like someone calling for help. I ran up the steps—yes, it was Granma. She was calling, "Won't somebody help me? O Lawd, have mercy!"

"Granma!" I shouted, banging on the door. I tried to open it, but it was locked.

"Who dat?" Granma shouted. "Jesus, thank you! Yuh done sent someone t' help."

"It's Carissa. The door won't open."

"Run round back. An' hurry!"

I raced to the end of the porch, jumped over the rail, and ran to the back. That door was locked, too, so I pushed open the window, pulled myself through, and dropped onto the floor of Granma's bedroom. There was Granma, in her nightgown, sprawled on the floor by her bed.

"What happened?" I cried. "Granma, what is it?"

"O Lawd, it hurts. It hurts so bad!"

"What?"

"Mah ankle. It's broken. Oh, it hurts!" Her left ankle looked twice as big as it should.

"How did it happen?"

"Git me dat slop jar f'um under de bed," she pleaded. "An' help me git on it."

Getting the slop jar was easy; the rest wasn't.

"What happened, Granma?" I asked when we were finished—and both embarrassed.

"I don' know. I got outta bed dis mornin' an' I think I musta caught mah foot under dat rag rug. I think I tried t' grab on to de end o' de bed, but I went down. Musta passed out, too. Ooow," she sobbed. "It hurt like de devil!"

"I'll run get Mama," I said. Then I noticed that

Granma was shivering. The room was icy. Granma hadn't been able to get up and start a fire. "Let me get you some covers," I said.

"Mah feet," she moaned. "They's frozen."

I found some socks and put them on her. Every time I touched her foot, she winced. Then I wrapped her in a quilt and went to the kitchen to stir up the fire in the cook stove. Soon I had a cup of hot tea for her. I couldn't get Granma up off the floor, but I managed to help her move enough so that she could lean against the side of her bed.

"I'm going for Mama," I told her. "Will you be all right?"

"Yes, but hurry!"

I started for home, then realized that Miss Alma and Ronnie Ray were just two houses down. I ran and pounded on their door.

Miss Alma appeared right away, her hair tied up in a head rag. She was doing her Saturday morning cleaning. "Why, Carissa," she exclaimed. "What are you doing here? What's the matter?"

"Granma! She fell down and broke her ankle. Mama sent me up to get her because she was supposed to be at our house to help with the wash, but she didn't come. She's on the floor, and I can't get her up."

"Ronnie Ray!" Miss Alma called. He came to the door. "Rachel's broken her ankle. Carissa was just up there. We got to go help her off the floor. You run tell your mama," she told me. "We'll go and look after your granma until you get back."

I ran all the way home and blurted out my news.

"O Lord, this is all I need," Mama exclaimed. "All these linens to be washed, and we aren't going to get one living thing done today." She plopped down at the table and put her hands over her face for a moment. Then she jumped up and grabbed her coat. "I'm going to Granma's. You run to town as fast as you can go. If you see someone in a wagon, in a car—anything—you stop them and ask if they'll give you a ride. Say it's an emergency and you have to get to town fast. Understand?"

"Yes, ma'am. What do I do in town?"

"Get Bailey. Tell him what happened. Tell him we have to get Miz Rachel to Swainsboro."

"To Dr. Porter?"

"Unless you know of a doctor any closer who sees colored patients."

"I could run get Deacon Braithwaite. He'd take us in his wagon."

"The Braithwaites went to Metter to see their kinfolk for Thanksgiving and won't be back until tomorrow. Run along now, as quick as you can. Alma and Ronnie Ray will know what to do until I get there. We'll keep your granma comfortable until you and Mr. Bailey come back."

I took off running. Delia Washington, in her yard hanging out sheets, looked at me, but I didn't stop. I passed half a dozen cabins. People were up and about, but no one was headed into town. "Please let there be someone," I prayed. "Let there be a wagon."

Soon, I had to stop and catch my breath; then I ran again. I came up behind Mr. and Mrs. Brown, walking slowly to town. "Where you goin' in such a hurry?" Mrs. Brown asked as I went by them.

I gasped, "Granma broke her ankle. Mama's gone to her place, and I'm going to town for help." Then I ran some more.

No wagon or automobile appeared, not even a man on a horse. I ran most of the way to Summit and burst through the back door of Satterwhite's Hardware.

Bailey was sharpening an ax. "What are *you* doin' here?" he asked.

I was doubled over, trying to catch my breath.

"What is it? Is somethin' wrong?"

When I could breathe, I told him what had happened and that we had to get Granma to Swainsboro.

I followed Bailey to the front of the store so he could talk to Mr. Satterwhite.

"Tell you what," Mr. Satterwhite said. "It's a slow morning. I can let Jimmy look after the store, and I'll take Aunt Rachel to Swainsboro. We can go the minute Jimmy gets back from the drug store. He just went out for a Co' Cola."

"That'd be right kind o' you, Mist' James. That's more than generous."

"Hell, Bailey. As hard as you work, if I can't do something for you and yours in your hour of need, it'd be right pitiful. You know what the Good Book says: 'Do unto others.'"

"That sho' is the truth. That's what it say."

Jimmy came through the front door with his Coca-Cola, and in two minutes, Bailey and I were sitting beside Mr. Satterwhite as his truck rumbled along the washboard surface of Canoochee Road.

Mama and the others had gotten Granma onto the bed and dressed. The men carried her to the truck and tried to get her into the cab, but she complained about the pain so much that they ended up bringing out a pallet and putting it in the truck bed. Mama got in back with her, and Bailey and I rode up front with Mr. Satterwhite again.

Mama was right about it taking all day. By the time we reached Swainsboro, Dr. Porter already had an office full of patients, so we had to wait our turn. Mr. Satterwhite went off to do some business and said he'd come back to take us home. "I never thought a white man would be so generous," Mama said.

At last, Dr. Porter was able to see Granma. When he was finished, he came out and said yes, she'd fractured her ankle, but it wasn't too bad. Still, she had to be in a cast for a few weeks, and she shouldn't stay by herself during that time.

"You know what this means," Mama announced, dropping into a chair. "Miz Rachel has to come live with us for a while." She didn't sound any too pleased about it.

I wasn't sure what to think. "What's wrong with that, Mama?" I asked.

"It just makes everything more . . . complicated," she answered.

"It'll be all right," Bailey said. "Won't be but for a little while."

"Where will she sleep?" I asked.

"That's what I mean," Mama said. "Our place is hardly big enough for the two of us. And you know how your granma and I sometimes disagree about things."

I was starting to see Mama's point. "Where *will* Granma sleep?" I asked again.

"In the bedroom with us. Unless you have a better idea."

"What about her bed?"

"I'll get it down to you," Bailey said. "Mr. Satterwhite'll let me bring it in his truck."

"You'd better not ask that man for too much," Mama warned. "You know what they say about wearing out your welcome."

"Don't you fret none, missuz. Mr. Satterwhite a good man. He won't mind."

And he didn't. In fact, he drove us home and even helped Bailey carry Granma into the house. Then I stayed with her while they went back to Granma's. Mama packed up some clothes for her, and the men took apart her bed and brought it back in the truck.

When Mama tried to pay Mr. Satterwhite for gasoline, he refused, and he told Bailey that he was giving him a full day's wages despite the hours he had missed.

We stood on our porch and waved at Mr. Satterwhite as he drove away. "Well, I never thought I'd see the day" was all Mama could say.

Miss Alma and Ronnie Ray showed up with a hot supper, and Mama was so grateful, she cried a little bit. Granma went to bed early. Mama said she was too tired for a bath, so after supper, when Bailey had gone to his shed, we sat near the fireplace, listening to the deep snoring that had begun ten minutes after Mama had told Granma good night.

"If she keeps that up all night, I'll never get any sleep," Mama fretted. "It sounds like a ten-pound bullfrog is loose in there."

I giggled.

"You won't think it's so funny come three o'clock in the morning and you're trying to sleep in the middle of that mess. We'll see how tired you'll be tomorrow, and all that washing to do. Who do you think is going to help me now that Miz Rachel is laid up?"

I hadn't thought of that.

"I don't know what we're going to do while Miz Rachel can't work," Mama went on. "She won't be bringing in any money for herself while she's crippled, and as long as she's with us, we'll have an extra mouth to feed. And who's going to pay her doctor bill?"

I hadn't thought about the money, either. No wonder Mama felt worried. So did I, now.

"I can stay out of school," I said. "I'll help you, Mama."

"Thank you, sugar. I hope you won't have to, but you're sweet to offer. I know I can count on you."

I was glad to know that Mama believed in me.

ELEVEN

Granma loved being waited on. Mama said she could understand that; after all, Granma had worked like a dog all her life, and who wouldn't enjoy just sitting in a rocking chair while other people cooked the food, washed the dishes, and kept the house clean?

Granma loved complaining even more. Nothing Mama did was right. The room was too hot or too cold, the corn bread was too brown or not brown enough, and I was either too loud and talkative or too quiet and moody.

Granma sat in her chair like a queen, making comments about everything Mama did, either scolding because Mama wouldn't sit and gossip to help pass the time or warning that unless she got some extra laundry jobs to do, we'd all starve. Dr. Porter had loaned Granma some crutches and showed her how to use them, but she didn't seem very interested in getting back on her feet. She could hobble from her bed to the rocking chair by the fireplace, but she said that getting down the back steps to the outhouse was out of the question, and she didn't know if she'd *ever* be able to "really walk by mahself again."

That had Mama frantic. "If she ends up moving in here permanently, they might just as well pack me up and deliver me to the lunatic asylum," she told me one afternoon as we took down clothes. It was now mid-December, and Granma had been with us two weeks. "I can't keep on waiting on her hand and foot while she passes the time finding fault with everything."

"What are you going to do?"

Mama finished folding one of Mrs. Davis's tea towels. "I didn't notice the tear in this one," she said. "I'll have to mend it before you iron it this evening." She put it to one side. "I'm going to ask Bailey his advice about your granma. He can't speed up her healing, but maybe a word from him can help change her attitude."

After supper that night, Bailey stayed in the house longer than usual while Mama helped Granma get into the bedroom and change into her nightclothes and I got started on the ironing. When Mama came out, she left the door halfway open. Then she took out Mrs.

Davis's tea towel to mend and said, "Mr. Bailey, why don't you tell us a story? Carissa told me about how Mr. Squirrel tried to save up sunshine in hickory nuts. It makes me smile every time I think about how he played the fool. You must know some other stories just as good."

"I might. What 'bout you, Carissa? You like a story, too?"

"Yes, sir," I said immediately. Listening to Bailey would help pass the time while I ironed. Ironing had become my job . . . and I had learned to hate it. It was tiresome having to heat the flatirons on the hearth, and they were so heavy that using them made my arms ache. Not only that, but I had to be careful not to burn myself or to get them too hot. If I did, they'd scorch the cloth and ruin it. I could iron flat things like pillowcases and tablecloths pretty well, but shirts still gave me trouble. I tried not to complain, because I knew Mama was depending on my help. I was also grateful that, so far, I'd been able to stay in school. There wasn't any time for playing when I got home, though. It was all work.

"A story?" Bailey said. "Let me think." He puffed on his pipe a moment, and then, "Oh, I got a good one. Y'all gonna like this one, sure.

"Once upon a time, back in Alabama, there was this couple, name o' Hetty and Silas. Hetty loved Silas, 'cause he was a good man, and faithful to her, and a hard worker. They'd already raised three young'uns, all grown up now and on they own. Everything was goin' on good, except they was jus' one fly in the buttermilk: Silas was the worst complainer you ever heard tell of. He complained about all kinds o' things—how the weather was too wet, or too dry, how his ol' hound dog Zeke couldn't scare up no 'coons no more, how seed potatoes cost too much, and how pecans brought in too little.

"Hetty had done put up with his complaints 'cause she loved him, but one day, she jus' done had enough. It was when Silas had taken a taste of her pound cake, and told her it had too much lemon flavorin' in it. 'I done made it the exact same way I always do,' she told him, but he said that couldn't be. Hetty knew right then what she would do."

"Excuse me, Mr. Bailey," Mama said. "Carissa, do you need me to dampen some more pillowcases?"

I felt the pile of laundry. "Yes, ma'am. The top ones are just about all dry."

Mama got the sprinkling bottle and went to work on the pillowcases. "Thank you for waiting," she told Bailey.

"Next mornin' after Silas went to work," Bailey continued, "Hetty cut half o' that pound cake and wrapped it in brown paper. She took a bottle of her best bread 'n' butter pickles, and she went down the road and through the swamp until she come to the cabin of Sister Zenobia, the root worker. Hetty knocked on the cabin door, and this spooky woman appeared, dressed in a long robe and wearin' a necklace made of animal bones. She invited Hetty inside.

"Hetty gave Sister Zenobia the cake and the pickles and explained 'bout Silas always complainin' about everything. Sister Zenobia listened, and then she said she got jus' the thing. She gave Hetty a tiny bottle with some yellow liquid in it, and she told her that that night, after Silas was asleep, to take some o' that and put a little drop on his lips, then sit back and wait to see what would happen. Then she gave her another bottle, this one with red liquid in it, and she said that when Silas done had enough of what was gon' happen to him, to put a drop o' the red liquid on his lips when he was sleep.

"'That's all?' Hetty asked.

"'That's all,' Sister Zenobia replied. ''Cept one thing. If you likes the way my conjure works, you come visit me again and bring me some o' them ham hocks 'n' greens you so famous for. Is it a deal?'

"So Hetty agreed, and that very night, after Silas fell asleep, she took a drop o' that yellow liquid and put it on his lips. He didn't notice a thing, jus' kept snorin' along."

"Ow!" I cried suddenly. I had been holding a pillowcase to keep it from slipping off the ironing board, and I had accidentally touched my hand with the flatiron.

"Did you hurt yourself?" Mama asked, jumping up.

"You burned bad?" Bailey asked.

I looked at my hand. There was a little red mark where the iron had gotten me. "I'm all right," I said.

"Dip a cloth in some water and hold it on the burn," Mama said. "I'll go on with the ironing."

I did what Mama said and sat down by Bailey.

"We'll try not to interrupt anymore," Mama said.

"That's all right," he said. "Next mornin', Hetty fixed Silas his breakfast, like always. She made him a pot o' coffee, jus' like she always did, same amount o' coffee and water, and poured him a big, hot cup.

"'That's the worst coffee I ever tasted!' Silas shouted. 'No flavor to it. Since when did you forget how to make coffee?'

"Hetty 'pologized, but she smiled to herself, thinkin' she'd wait now and see what would happen. Turn out nothin' did—until next mornin'. She got up to cook breakfast and opened the can o' coffee beans to grind 'em, and the can was completely empty! Now, that was strange, 'cause Silas himself had brought home two full pounds o' beans jus' three days earlier.

"When Silas sat down to eat, Hetty put the food out, but she didn't pour no coffee.

"'Where's my coffee?' he demanded.

"'Ain't no coffee,' Hetty said.

"'Don't mess with me,' Silas warned. 'They's almost two pounds o' coffee in that can right there.' He got up to look, but Hetty was right: there weren't no coffee anywhere in the house.

"So Silas sat down to eat his fatback and grits.

'These is the lumpiest grits I ever tried to eat!' he cried. 'When did you forget how to cook grits?'

"Hetty 'pologized and told him she made the grits jus' the same way she been makin' 'em the last twenty-three years, but she would try harder tomorrow.

"Next mornin', she got up to cook again, and they warn't no grits—not even one little grit—in the grits jar. And still no coffee in the coffee can, neither.

"Silas sat down to eat, and he asked, 'Where's my coffee?'

"'Ain't no coffee.'

"'Where's my grits?'

"'Ain't no grits.'

"Silas was mighty aggravated now, and he stormed around searchin' for some coffee and grits somewhere in the cabin. 'Course he didn't find none, so he sat down to eat the cornpone Hetty had cooked for him.

"'This is the driest cornpone I ever ate!' Silas shouted. 'When did you forget how to cook a pone without overbakin' it?'

"Hetty said she done made it jus' the same way as always, but she was sorry it didn't taste good to him. Silas stormed out o' the house saying he wondered how he was still alive, after sufferin' through such bad cookin' all these years.

"But Hetty, she jus' sang to herself all day long."

Mama chuckled and nodded at Bailey. He smiled at her and nodded back.

Something was going on.

"Next morning, Silas sat down to eat," Bailey went on. "'Where's my coffee?' he shouted.

"'Ain't no coffee.'

"Hetty put down his plate. Nothin' on it 'cept a piece o' fried fatback.

"'Where're my grits?'

"'Ain't no grits.'

"'Fatback all they is?'

"'All they is,' Hetty agreed.

"'Didn't you go to the store?'

"'All sold out.'

"So Silas went on to work. He was mighty hungry, 'cause all he got in his belly was some fatback. All the way to work, Silas was mumblin' and complainin' to himself. 'What a awful job I got,' he thought. 'Hard, dangerous work, and nobody appreciates what I do. Man work himself to the bone year after year and hardly got anything to show for it.'"

Bailey stopped to put some more tobacco in his pipe. "How's that hand?" he asked.

I had already forgotten about it. "All right," I said, taking a look at the place. "Mama, I can iron again if you want."

"There's only a few more to do," she said. It was true. Mama could iron a lot faster than I could. She already had a pile of neatly pressed pillowcases and tea towels. "You could put the kettle on to boil and stir up the fire, though. A cup of tea would taste real good before bedtime."

While I filled the kettle, Bailey continued with the story. "Silas got to the sawmill, and instead o' lots of men goin' in to work, he saw 'em all standin' around by the front gate. 'What's goin' on?' he wondered. He went up to the gate and saw a big ol' lock on it. 'Why's the gate locked?' Silas asked.

"'Owner musta gone outta business,' his friend Jake told him. 'Closed up in the middle o' the night and took off somewheres. Guess he was losin' too much money, price of pine bein' down like it is. I reckon he didn't have money for tomorrow's payroll, and he afraid to face us.'

"'But what about my job?' Silas cried.

"'Ain't no job,' Jake said.

"And it sho' appeared there warn't. All the men looked at that locked gate for 'bout another half hour, and then one by one they started leavin', headin' home to tell they womenfolk that the mill done closed and hard times had come for sure.

"Silas walked home and threw himself down on the bed. 'What you doin' home from your job in the middle of the mornin'?' Hetty asked him.

"'Ain't no job' was all he would say.

"Come suppertime, Silas wouldn't eat. Wouldn't talk. Jus' lay on the bed, starin' at the ceiling, wonderin' why everything in his life had gone to the bad. Hetty watched him close and pretended like she was all upset, too, but in her mind, she knew that Sister Zenobia's conjure been workin' its work.

"That night, before he went to bed, Silas got to inspectin' himself in the lookin' glass. 'I hate my nose,' he complained. 'Always have. Never have liked the way it all spread out. Wish I had me a narrow nose, instead.'

"It was all Hetty could do not to bust out laughin', 'cause she knew what was comin'. Instead, she said, 'You got a perfect, handsome nose—a proper colored man's nose, and there's not one thing in this world wrong with it. Now, you quit your complainin' and be glad you got a nose.'

"Silas jus' hmmphed and wouldn't listen. He went to bed without sayin' another word to Hetty. Next mornin', she woke up first, but she lay in the bed with her eyes closed and pretended she was still asleep. Finally, she heard Silas get up and stumble round the room like he always did, and then she opened her eyes jus' a little bit and saw him standin' in front of the chest of drawers, and then she saw him look in the mirror.

"They say you could hear that man scream four counties away. 'My nose!' he yelled. 'My poor nose! What done happened to my beautiful nose?'"

Mama laughed out loud. "I saw that coming," she said.

"Me, too," I added. I looked at the bedroom door, wondering if we were disturbing Granma. Then all at once I understood everything—why Bailey had stayed around after supper, why Mama had asked him to tell a story, and why he had chosen to tell about Silas and Hetty. I was so pleased with myself that I laughed, too.

And I could hardly wait to find out what happened next.

"You ladies are way ahead o' me," Bailey said.

"Please finish," Mama told him.

"Where was I?"

"Silas's nose," I said.

"Oh, yeah. 'My nose!' Silas shouted. 'Where is my beautiful nose?'

"'What's all the ruckus?' Hetty asked, sittin' up in the bed. 'What are you shoutin' about?'

"'My nose is gone. Look!'

"Hetty looked. 'You's right,' she said. 'Ain't no nose—jus' two teensy little holes to breathe through.'

"'What am I gon' do?' wailed Silas. 'Oh, my nose, my handsome nose! Gone. Gone. Gone!'

"'Your *handsome* nose?' Hetty asked. 'I thought I heard you complainin' 'bout what a ugly nose you got. I'd a thought you'd be glad to be rid of it.'

"'I didn't know what I was sayin',' Silas cried. 'I'd do anything to have my old nose back. I never appreciated it like I should.'

"'What about your job?' Hetty asked.

"'Oh, my job!' moaned Silas. 'It was the best job I ever had.'

"'And what about all the other stuff you been complainin' about lately? Like my cooking.'

"'You's the best cook in the state. Oh, what I wouldn't give for a cup o' your coffee, and a plate full o' your grits and cornpone!'

"Hetty knew then she had Silas right where she

wanted him. 'You come back to bed and try to get you a little more rest,' she advised him. 'You look like a whupped hound. Best thing for you would be 'bout another hour's sleep. Tell you what: While you rest, I'll make you the best breakfast you ever ate.'

"'How can you, without no coffee or grits or cornmeal?'

"'You leave that to me. I reckon I can scare somethin' up.'

"The minute Hetty heard him snorin' good, she grabbed for that bottle o' red liquid. She smeared some on Silas's lips and then she went to fix some food. When she got to the coffee can, she found it full of the freshest, brownest coffee beans she ever saw, so she ground up some and got a pot goin'. The grits jar was full, and so was the bin o' cornmeal, so she was able to git a big meal prepared.

"When Silas woke up, there was his nose, jus' as good as new, maybe a little flatter than before, but he said he liked it better than the old one. And there was his breakfast, and he told Hetty that it was the best cup o' coffee he ever drank, and the best dish o' grits he ever ate, and the best piece o' cornpone he ever put in his mouth. After he ate all that up, he said he was still hungry and asked if Hetty still had a slice of that scrumptious lemon pound cake left. He was jus' sayin' how it was the best pound cake Hetty ever made when his friend Jake came knockin' on the door with the news that the sawmill had done reopened that mornin'.

The owner hadn't never planned to shut down for good, said Jake. He'd been on his way to the mill yesterday mornin', but when he got to the bridge across the river, he found that a runaway barge had done rammed the bridge and collapsed it. Everybody knew there weren't another way across for fifteen miles in either direction, so he set out south to get to the next bridge, but by the time he got to the mill, it was evenin' and everybody had already left.

"'We still got our jobs?' Silas asked.

"'Yeah, and the boss gon' pay us time and half for yesterday, to make up for the inconvenience and worry,' said Jake.

"So Silas scrambled to get dressed, and Hetty packed him a big dinner to take, and he went off that day happier than he been in a long time. Before he left, he turned to Hetty and said, 'I reckon I owe you an apology. I been thinkin' about it, and I can see now I been complainin' too much. I'm glad for what I have, and if I ever go to complainin' again, I hope that my—'

"Hetty stopped him before he called down a curse on himself. 'I forgive you,' she told him. 'It's a good feeling to be satisfied with what we got. And I's satisfied with you.' Then she kissed him on the cheek, right in front of Jake, and sent the men off to work.

"As he was walkin' out of the yard, Silas turned back and called out to Hetty, 'You reckon you could cook up some of your ham hocks 'n' greens for supper? They's my favorite.'

"'That's jus' what I had in mind,' said Hetty.

"'Cook a double pot.'

"'I think I will,' she said. 'Now, get on t' work.'

"And they both lived together for a lot more years, in peace and contentment," Bailey finished. "And that's the end."

"That was a wonderful story," Mama said. "And it makes a good point, too. I'm glad Carissa heard it."

I was ready to go along with Mama and Bailey's plan. "Mama! I don't complain about your cooking."

"No, but you find your mess to moan about."

"Dat was a mighty fine story," came Granma's voice from the bedroom. "You shoulda been a preacher, Mr. Bailey."

Mama and Bailey looked at each other and grinned. "Why, Miz Rachel, I thought you were asleep all this time," Mama called to her. "If I'd known Bailey's story was going to keep you awake, I would never have asked him to tell it."

"I beg your pardon, Miz Rachel," Bailey added. "I didn't mean to run on so long with a triflin' tale. But I's glad you enjoyed it."

We could hear movement in the next room, and in a moment, there was Granma standing at the door, pulling on her shawl over her nightgown. I noticed right away that she didn't have her crutch. Although she was holding on to the doorframe, she was standing perfectly well on both legs, as if her left ankle hardly bothered her at all.

"Triflin'?" she asked. "With folks complainin' an' moanin' all de time 'bout how dey don't like dis an' dey don't like dat? 'Bout drives me crazy de way folks carries on, 'specially when dey got so much to be thankful fer. Whole heap o' folks I could name what ought to hear *dat* story."

"You're right generous," Bailey said.

"Jus' tellin' de truf de way it is. Now I am goin' to bed. Yes, sir, yuh done give us *all* a lot to think about," she said, giving me a significant look. With that, she turned away and pushed the bedroom door shut behind her.

Mama and Bailey looked at each other again, and Mama laughed as quietly as she could until tears ran down her face. Watching her trying to keep quiet was the funniest thing.

"You and Bailey planned all of that," I said. "I had it figured out."

"Shh!" Mama told me. "Your granma would never forgive us."

"How did you figure it out?" Bailey whispered to me.

"Mama left the bedroom door open," I whispered back. "She wanted Granma to hear everything."

The three of us enjoyed some tea, and then Bailey went to his shed.

Beginning the next day, Granma never complained about another thing as long as she stayed with us. She even told Mama at every meal how much she liked her cooking.

Twelve

Two weeks before Christmas, on a Monday afternoon, I helped Mama deliver clean laundry, since Granma couldn't make the long walk to town. Our last stop was at Mrs. Davis's. We turned left at the corner of First Avenue and College Street and came to the side door of the big white house with the wraparound porch and lots of fancy woodwork.

Mama knocked, and Mrs. Davis answered right away. She came down the steps and stood with us by our wagon.

"Good afternoon, Lorena," Mrs. Davis said. "My, it's cold out here. Hello, Carissa. I don't get to see *you* very often. Remind me to get you a ginger cake before you leave."

"Good afternoon, Mrs. Davis," I replied, as Mama had taught me.

"You'll want to hurry home," the lady continued. "We'll surely have a frost tonight. Lorena, I pray you have Mother's Belgian lace doilies in that load. I don't recall giving them to you, but that's the only place they can be. I can't find them anywhere."

Mama shook her head. "No, ma'am. You didn't give me any doilies. I always wash them separately, in warm water with a mild soap, but I didn't do them this time around."

"You're quite certain? I've been searching everywhere. They simply *must* be with you. I almost had John ride out to your place to ask, but it's such a long way out there. Maybe you forgot. Open the parcel and we'll check."

"I will, but I'm sure they aren't here."

"If they're lost, I'll just die. My father bought those for Mother on his first European trip. He told her they were handmade by nuns in the cloister of Ste. Marie Madeleine in Bruges, Belgium. The most intricate, delicate lacework you'll ever see . . ."

"I know," Mama agreed, as if she'd heard all about it many times. She lifted one layer of linen after another. "They aren't here, Miz Davis."

"Perhaps you left them at your house. Maybe you dropped them somewhere and didn't notice. I just hope they're not in some dusty corner in your—"

Mama got very still. Then she said, "The corners of my house are as clean as any broom and mop can make them. They're as clean as anything in *your* place."

Mrs. Davis stared at Mama. "What did you say to me?"

"I said that my house, no matter what you might think, is just as clean as yours. That's what I said." Mama was looking Mrs. Davis right in the eye, something she had told me never to do when speaking to a white person.

A little knot of ice formed in my stomach. I was used to seeing Mama quarrel with people like Mrs. Washington, but I'd never seen her in a fight with a white person before. "Please don't let this happen," I prayed silently. If Mama tangled with Mrs. Davis, something terrible would happen. I was sure of it. White people could make big trouble if they wanted to.

"Do you know what I really think?" the woman shot back. "I believe you *stole* Mother's doilies and that they're at your house this very minute. I think I'll send John out to your place this evening so he can have a look for himself."

"He can waste his time if he wants to, but he won't find anything, because they aren't there. They're somewhere in *your* house, where *you* misplaced them. I don't want your silly doilies, and I am not a thief!"

"How dare you speak to me like that? If you were from around *here,* Lorena, you'd know your place. No colored girl has ever insulted me like this, and I assure you it won't happen again. You are dismissed, and I won't be paying you today. I'll keep my money, although it won't begin to cover the cost of Mother's doilies."

She grabbed her laundry and hurried to the door. Before she went into the house, she looked over her shoulder and declared, "I know my friends will be interested to learn your *true* nature, Lorena. I'm sure they'll want to find a more reliable girl to do their washing." She slammed the door, and I heard it lock.

Mama stood silent and rigid, like a statue. "Come on," she said at last. "It's getting cold."

That was a long, quiet walk home through the gathering dusk. When we got to our gate, Mama told me to put the wagon up and bring some kindling so she could build up the fire in the stove.

For an hour I'd been trying to think of the right thing to say, something to make Mama feel better. "I'll bet our corners are even cleaner than Mrs. Davis's!" I cried. My words sounded silly to me the moment I said them, but Mama smiled and told me to move along if I wanted a hot supper.

As I brought in the kindling, I heard Granma say, "So de lady make one offhand remark 'bout yo' housekeepin', an' yuh sasses her to her *face?*"

"Miz Rachel, I've had a bad day, and I don't need this mess now," Mama warned. "First the woman suggested that I had lost her mother's whatever kind of fancy doilies they are, and then she accused me of stealing them. Am I supposed to stand there and take it?"

I felt confused. When Poppy sassed Jeralynn, she got a bloody mouth, and Mama told her just to keep quiet when ignorant people tried to mess with her. But Mama hadn't kept quiet when Mrs. Davis accused her of stealing. What *was* a person supposed to do?

Granma pushed herself up from her rocker and limped to the stove. She got right up in Mama's face. "Yes, ma'am, yuh's supposed to take it! No matter how much it hurt. No matter how wrong it is. 'Cause dat's de way it is round here, an' dey ain't *nothin'* nobody kin do about it. Dat ol' hen didn't mean nothin' by it noways. You jus' can't go gettin' all fired up 'bout every person's foolish remarks, 'specially a white person's."

Now it was Mama's turn. "I pray that you weren't always as pitiful as you are now. What has life done to you to drain you of every ounce of pride? Are you just going to let folks stomp on you like you were a palmetto bug?"

"Dere yuh go wid dat pride thing again! I told yuh dat a colored woman can't afford it."

"I'd rather be without a job, I'd rather be hungry and begging on the street, than throw away the one thing no one can take from me!"

What would Mama have done in Poppy's place when Jeralynn called her a funny little clown? Maybe you were supposed to fight back if you were strong enough to have a chance of winning. If not, maybe you were supposed to take it. I saw what happened to Poppy for fighting with Jeralynn and Etta Mae, but I was proud of Mama for standing up to Mrs. Davis.

"Den it look like yuh done got yo' wish, don't it?" Granma went on. "Yuh ain't got no job wid Miz Davis, an' by de time she get through talkin' 'bout *you* round town, yuh ain't gon' have no other jobs, neither. Den you an' dis poor child'll be comin' up de road to live wid me."

"I can't talk about this anymore. Let me get this meal cooked before Mr. Bailey gets here and expects his food. If it weren't for him, I swear I don't know what we'd do."

Supper that night was tense. Bailey came in, sensed a storm, and did what he could to take our minds off our troubles. Right after we ate, Granma went to bed and I was ordered to do my homework. Mama asked Bailey for a private word outside.

When she came inside, she dropped into her chair by the fire and fell asleep instantly. I finished my homework, put a quilt over Mama, and got myself to bed as quietly as I could. It seemed best just to let her be.

As it turned out, we did lose some laundry work. Mrs. Davis was a "big sow in a small pen," as Mama put it, and she spoke to some of her friends who were also our customers. The following Saturday, when we went to town to pick up dirty laundry, both Mrs. Pitts and Mrs. Coleman informed Mama that they were sorry but they needed "a more reliable girl" to do their work, and that Delia Washington would be their washwoman from now on.

Mama almost had a fit on Monday when she saw Mrs. Washington in her yard, singing over her kettle of boiling linens. "That's *my* work she stole from me," Mama fumed. "If she wants it, let her have it. Miz Pitts and Miz Coleman are going to be sorry they dropped me when they see what a sorry job that woman does with their rags."

But we still needed work, and Mama had to go from back door to back door along the streets of Summit, asking white women if they needed a laundry girl. She was lucky. With Christmas coming up, some ladies wanted extra help and gave Mama their work.

Granma could help with folding and mending, but she still couldn't do much. Now Mama needed me to stay home to help. She said she hated that I had to miss school, but work came first. Miss Johnson promised to send my lessons; she said I was so far ahead that a couple weeks' absence wouldn't hurt.

I wished I could be in school, but there was nothing to be done about it. Mama and I stayed busy bleaching tablecloths and napkins, washing and ironing sheets and pillowcases, and starching and ironing dresses and men's shirts. Bailey was working extra-long hours, too, and he gave Mama more money. But Mama had to pay Dr. Porter for setting Granma's ankle, and then Granma came down with pneumonia, and that meant the cost of the doctor's house call and medicine. With Christmas just a few days away, we were down to nearly nothing.

One thing made those days bearable: I just knew that come Christmas morning, the green bicycle I had seen in Durden's window would be mine. I didn't know how, but I knew that Bailey would make it possible.

The weekend before Christmas, Bailey said he had business to attend to down in Stillmore. He was gone from Saturday morning, when he went to work, until Sunday evening. He didn't say why he was going, and he seemed sad when he came home.

On Christmas Eve, Bailey came home later than usual, and Mama started fretting, but when he arrived, he was in a cheerful mood. He whistled as he brought in extra wood and refilled the water bucket. After supper, he gave us a surprise: he'd cut some holly branches in the woods and stuck them into a bucket of wet sand to make a little Christmas tree. He opened a sack of popping corn, Mama popped some over the fire, and we sat and strung what we didn't eat. Then we decorated our little tree.

Before I went to bed, I set out three small packages that I had wrapped in brown paper. They were hand-sewn handkerchiefs for Mama, Granma, and Bailey, each with their initial embroidered in the corner. Nothing anywhere looked like a present for me, but in the morning, the green bicycle would be there. It had to be.

When I awoke, the coffee was brewing and Mama

was bustling about in the next room. Granma was still sleeping quietly; if she had snored during the night, I hadn't heard her. The air was chilly, so I knew it was cold outside. I slipped out of bed, pulled on my sweater and socks, and peeped out the window, hoping for snow. Of course there wasn't any. It hardly ever snowed.

In the kitchen, Mama was setting the table. "Merry Christmas," she greeted me. "Did you sleep all right?"

"Yes, ma'am."

"Aren't you going to wish me a Merry Christmas?"

I went to her. "Merry Christmas, Mama."

I noticed some packages on the table that hadn't been there last night. The bicycle was too big to bring inside, I realized, so it was probably on the porch, or out back.

Just then, Bailey knocked on the back door, a large paper sack in his hand. We got Granma up, and we ate breakfast. Mama had made cinnamon buns loaded with sticky syrup and pecans.

Then we opened our gifts. Bailey took four oranges and some peppermint sticks out of the sack. For me, there were new long stockings that Granma had knitted, a hand-me-down sweater Mama had received from Mrs. Rountree, a lady she washed for, and a new cold-weather dress. The grownups opened their handkerchiefs and exclaimed over my sewing. They had not given each other anything.

"I got one more thing for Carissa," Bailey said, heading for the back door. I sat up, smoothed my sweater and hair, and gazed expectantly at the back door.

But when Bailey reappeared, he held a package in his hands. "Thought you might like this," he said.

If it wasn't the green bicycle, it could have no interest for me. Nothing mattered now, not even Christmas. But I had to be polite—pretend to be excited and grateful. I tore at the gay Christmas paper. The shape of the package told me it was a book, a thick, heavy one. When the paper was gone, in my lap sat a big book bound in red. *Stories from the Thousand and One Nights,* it said on the cover.

"Look inside," Bailey urged. "It has pictures."

Opening it gently, the way Miss Johnson had taught me to handle a new book, I paged to a color picture of a man dressed in baggy purple pants; his yellow shoes had turned-up toes. A bright red vest partially covered his bare brown chest, and on his head was a white turban. He was hanging from the claws of a gigantic bird. "Sinbad seized by the Roc," read the caption.

"I asked Miz Johnson could she recommend a book," Bailey said. "She told me this one. Ordered it for me. I hope you like it."

That's when I burst into tears. Covering my eyes with both hands, I cried for all I was worth. The book slid off my lap and landed on the floor with a thud.

"What in the world?" Mama said. "Mr. Bailey paid a lot of money for that. Don't tell me you don't like it!"

"I do," I answered miserably. "It's the most wonderful book I ever got."

"Then what's the matter?"

"Take down your hands," Bailey said gently. "Wipe your eyes." Mama gave me the new handkerchief I had made her. "Now, look at me, honey. . . . It's the green bicycle, ain't it?"

I could only nod, and then the tears came again.

"Well, I never!" Mama exclaimed.

"Shh, missuz," Bailey said. "It's all right." He patted my knee. "I understand," he said.

"I love the book," I said. "It's just that—" I couldn't find any more words.

"It's okay to be disappointed," Bailey said. "Even on Christmas Day."

Just then Poppy came to the door, eager to see the new bicycle I had told her a hundred times I was getting.

❧

After New Year, I was able to return to school. Now that the holidays were over, Mama had less laundry to do, and she could get along without my help during the day. I wasn't excited about going back, though. Christmas had left me with an empty feeling. Nothing really good could happen now. Mama was right: We would always be stuck in Summit, and life would never be anything but a long, hard uphill climb.

Poppy tried her best to cheer me up, and we did have some fun times together, riding bikes. But then I would remember that it was Bailey's bike I was riding, not my own. And what would happen if Bailey ever *did* go away to live somewhere else? He would take his bicycle with him, leaving me with nothing.

Mama found a job cooking in one of the railroad hotels in town. She was up and gone before dawn, and Granma and I would awaken to find our breakfast being kept warm on the back of the cook stove. Now I had to get myself washed up and dressed without Mama standing over me to urge me along. Bailey would tap on the back door each day to make sure I was out of bed. That helped, especially during the dark, cold mornings of January.

By the end of the month, Granma was healed up enough to go home. Bailey carved her a cane—which we didn't think she'd accept, but she did—and borrowed a wagon to take home her bed and clothes.

Mama was so tired every day when she got home that many nights Bailey and I cooked supper for ourselves. Mama would sit by the fire while I washed the dishes and tidied up the kitchen before turning to my homework. She was too exhausted from cooking all day long to check my lessons. Often, before I had finished them, she would start to nod off. Bailey would whisper a good night and tiptoe out the back door. Then I would rouse Mama and send her to bed. It felt like I was the one taking care of her now.

One Saturday morning in early February, as we were starting out for Summit, Mama stopped and stared at something on Delia Washington's clothesline. She pushed through Mrs. Washington's gate, headed to the side yard, and went right to the clothesline. Even from the road, I knew what she was looking at: Mrs. Davis's Belgian lace doilies.

Mama went up on the porch and hammered on the door. When Mrs. Washington opened it, she looked surprised to see Mama. They hadn't spoken a word to each other since the incident with the scuppernongs.

Part of me wished Mama would just leave things alone. Hadn't we had enough upset about the doilies already? But another part was interested to see what would happen. I didn't think it was going to be anything nice.

"Yes?" Mrs. Washington asked, like she was talking to some stranger.

"Do those doilies out there belong to Miz Davis?" Mama asked.

"What if they do? Ain't no business of yours."

"Do they?" Mama demanded.

"I reckon. She give 'em to me to wash."

"When did she start giving them to you?"

"Now, jus' a minute! I ain't got to answer any of your—"

"When?"

"I don' know. Before Christmas."

"That woman lost her precious doilies way back at Thanksgiving and accused me of stealing them!" Mama shouted. "She fired me from being her laundry woman and got a bunch of other women in town to do the same. She made up lies about me. And now I see she found her doilies but doesn't have the common decency to come apologize for her false accusations."

I could feel my heart beating fast. Mama was right. Mrs. Davis was no good.

Mrs. Washington had managed to pull herself together. "I don't know nothin' 'bout any o' that. All I know is what she done told me."

"And what was that?"

"That ever since you started workin' for her, she began missin' things—towel here, pillowcase there. She said the last straw was when you spent a day at her place cleanin' some carpets and the next day her gold thimble was gone. She said you denied stealin' it, but she never did trust you none after that. I don't know nothin' about them doilies. Now, if you will excuse me, I got work to do."

Mrs. Davis was saying that Mama stole things! I wanted to run to the clothesline, grab the doilies, throw them down, and grind them into the dirt. That would show Mrs. Davis! I took three steps before I stopped myself. Ruining the doilies would only make things worse.

"That woman is a low-down snake!" Mama cried. "I never stole a thimble from her. If she missed it, which I doubt she did, she never said one word to me about it."

"You *did* go clean them carpets, though," Mrs. Washington said smugly. "I heard you tellin' Alma Johnson about it at Hall's store. You said what a pretty pattern her front parlor carpet got on it—pink and blue roses."

"Yes, I did clean some carpets for her, but—"

"I guess it her word 'gainst yours, then."

"She never told me her thimble was missing!"

"That between you and Miz Davis. Now, I got to tend to my work. She give me a lot o' Mr. John's shirts to iron. Please excuse me."

She started to close the door, but Mama put her foot against it. "I'm not a thief. What that woman told you is a lie, and so was her accusation that I stole her precious doilies. If you believe her over me, you're a liar, too."

"No I ain't, either. The only thing I am is sorry that I got to live next door to you. I tried to be neighborly, but they's some folks you jus' can't be nice to. Your mouth done got you in trouble ever since you came here, and I can see it still is. Now, get off my place and let me do my work."

I hated Mrs. Washington. She had no right to talk to Mama that way. But she was telling Mama the same thing Mama had told Poppy and me: You get in trouble when you talk back, or when you stand up for yourself. I was puzzled about why Mama would tell me one thing, but do something else herself.

"I'll be glad to leave after you pay me for my hen your dog killed," Mama said. "You told me then you'd pay for it, but I guess that was a lie, just like the ones you and Miz Davis have been spreading about me."

"Wait there," Mrs. Washington said, and went inside. She came back and threw a handful of coins right at Mama. "You want 'em? Take 'em. Then take yourself off my porch." And she slammed the door.

I watched Mama stand there a moment; then she turned on her heel and walked down the steps toward me. "Let's go," she said.

On the way to Summit, I wanted to ask all the questions that had been running around in my mind, but I was afraid to say anything. Mama looked angry enough to explode. I didn't want to set her off.

In Summit, Mama turned left onto First Avenue, and suddenly I knew what she had in mind. I couldn't stay quiet anymore. "What are you going to do, Mama?" I asked.

"Tell Mrs. Davis to her face," she said. "Enough is enough." She kept going.

"Stop," I pleaded.

"What is it?"

"When Poppy had the fight with Jeralynn and Etta Mae, you told her not to mess with them ever again. You made me promise not to help her if she did. But you don't let anybody mess with *you*. You stand up for yourself, even when it makes trouble. What's right?"

"This isn't the time to stop and explain things," Mama began. She looked around to see if anyone was nearby. "Let's wait till we're back home."

"Why do you have to talk to Mrs. Davis? I don't want you to fight anymore."

"All right," Mama said. "Let me see if I can explain this. . . . You and Poppy have to learn that the world is full of people who want to pick at you for the littlest things, like the clothes you're wearing or the way you do your hair."

"Jeralynn teased me about my ears."

"That's right. And there's not a thing you can do about them, so it's best to let it be when someone teases you. But other times, you have to stand up for yourself, like when someone attacks your character."

"I don't understand."

Mama thought for a moment. "I mean, attacks the kind of person you are on the inside. Like whether you're honest or not. Like whether you have the right to speak your mind. Then you have to say something. You have to learn to choose what battles you're going to fight."

"You have to fight Mrs. Davis? She already made you lose work."

"She attacked my character, sugar. I can't let that go, no matter what it costs."

"I'm afraid."

Mama put her arm around me. "So am I. But this is something I have to do. Understand?"

"Yes," I answered. I did understand better now, but I still wished we could turn around and go home.

At Mrs. Davis's house, Mama went to the side door and knocked. Mrs. Davis opened the door. "Lorena," she said. "I'm surprised to see *you* here."

"Miz Davis, I have something to say to you, and I need for you to listen."

"I'm *so* pleased," Mrs. Davis said, smiling. "Some of them said you'd never apologize, but I told them you're a good girl at heart, and sooner or later you'd see you were wrong and come and make it right."

"No, ma'am, that's not it." Mama kept her voice low. "I don't have anything to apologize for. I saw your doilies hanging on Delia Washington's clothesline this morning. That means I never took them. It means *you* lost them and accused *me* of stealing. When you realized you were wrong, you didn't have the courtesy to let me know."

I felt myself trembling.

Mrs. Davis's smile had faded, and she was looking at Mama through cold eyes, but she said nothing.

Mama kept talking. "Furthermore, I found out that you've been spreading lies about me, saying that I stole a gold thimble from this house. Maybe you had to make up a lie to cover your own mistakes. You've already lost me some other jobs, so there's nothing else you can do to me. Or maybe there is. But whatever happens, *I* know that *you* are the liar, not me. And that's all I have to say."

All this time, Mama had kept her voice down. She hadn't yelled or made any threats, but she had looked Mrs. Davis straight in the eye. I had never felt so proud to have her as my mama as I did right then.

Mrs. Davis still didn't say anything.

"Come on," Mama told me. "Let's go."

"You'll be sorry!" Mrs. Davis suddenly shouted after Mama. "Smart-mouthed nigger!"

All at once, I understood why Poppy had attacked Jeralynn and Etta Mae. There were some things you couldn't ignore.

I began to turn around, ready to sass Mrs. Davis, but Mama seemed to understand my intentions. She took me by the shoulder and pushed me along. "Just keep going," she said. "There's no use wasting your breath on a woman like her."

Maybe Mama was right, but she couldn't keep me from thinking, and my thoughts about Mrs. Davis were not nice at all.

THIRTEEN

I waited for Bailey on the porch that evening so I could tell him what had happened and Mama wouldn't have to. In silence, she put supper on the table for us and then said she had a sick headache and had to go to bed. The next morning, she didn't even get up but told me to get myself ready and go on to church with Bailey.

When we got home, Mama was up and dressed, but there was no dinner made. She said she was too tired to do anything but sit. That's all she said. It was a pleasant late-winter day, so Bailey suggested she go onto the porch and enjoy the fresh air while we warmed up some food.

I was worried. Mama had been upset before, but she would knock pots and pans together or rant about whatever it was that was bothering her. I was used to her being noisy when she was angry. Her silence was scary.

After dinner, Bailey suggested we go for a walk in the country, seeing as it was a beautiful afternoon. Mama said she couldn't, she was too worn out. But he finally convinced her, and soon we were on our way out toward the sand hills, where Bailey had taken Poppy and me last fall. He kept pointing out things—the pale green fiddleheads of ferns poking through the ground, a pair of cardinals looking for nest-building materials, the paw prints of a raccoon in the soft earth by the edge of the road.

After a while, Bailey led us off the road. He had us sit down near what looked like an animal burrow. A pile of sand was mounded in front of the hole, and there were jumbled scratch marks everywhere, as if something had been digging.

"What kind of animal did that?" I asked.

"Let's us be quiet and wait, and maybe we'll see," Bailey said.

"Sounds good to me," Mama said. "That walk wore me out." She leaned back against one of the scrub oaks. "It feels so good to sit here in the sunshine and just do nothing."

We sat and waited. Mama closed her eyes, and in a few minutes, she was asleep. The longer I sat, however, the more interested I became in the scene around me. Ants and beetles went about their business right in front of my feet. A mockingbird flew from bush to bush, checking his territory.

"Look," Bailey whispered after a while. He touched Mama on the shoulder, and she roused. "Quiet now," he warned. "Nothin' to be frightened of. Jus' sit tight."

From the dark mouth of the burrow emerged the wedge-shaped head of a diamondback rattlesnake. It looked immense, with a head as big as a pancake. I felt my heart skip a beat. Rattlers were even more dangerous than cottonmouths, Mama said. They had bad tempers, and you couldn't ever tell when they might strike.

I tried to stand up, and so did Mama, but Bailey grasped each of us by the shoulder and held us firmly in place. "Don't move."

The snake stopped partway out, its forked black tongue flicking. I told myself that if it came toward me, nobody—not even Bailey—was going to keep me there. I would be running backward as fast as I could go. But the snake came out of the hole and moved off to our right without seeming to notice us. I could see that it really wasn't all that big, maybe as long as Miss Johnson's yardstick. That didn't matter; it had still terrified me. But now that I was safe, I almost collapsed with relief. My forehead and armpits were wet, and I was breathing hard.

"He's a beauty, isn't he?" Bailey asked.

How could he think that about a snake? "It might have come right over here and bitten us, and we'd be dead!"

"Have you lost your mind?" Mama asked him. "Bringing us where a poison snake could bite us? You just shaved ten years off of my life. As if I don't already have enough to worry about." She stood up and looked around at the ground. Maybe she wanted to be sure that the rattler really was gone.

"That snake ain't studyin' no people," Bailey answered calmly. "He got other business on his mind. You two warn't scared, was you?"

"Yes!" I cried. "Why didn't you tell us it's a snake hole?"

"'Cause it *ain't* a snake hole."

"A snake came out of it," Mama said.

"Sho' did. But Mr. Rattler didn't make that hole. Jus' borrowed it. Now, let's watch some more."

"Can't we go home?" I asked. I was hearing and seeing rattlesnakes everywhere. Surely, one was going to slither out of nowhere, open his jaws, clamp onto my leg, and kill me dead.

"Jus' a little while longer. Watch."

"For another snake to come out?" Mama challenged.

"Probably not. But somethin' else might."

Sure enough, another head appeared at the opening. It was attached to a rounded sandy brown shell.

"A turtle!" I said.

"No, a tortoise. It's like a turtle, but it don't live in the water. It's a gopher tortoise. Nice big one, too. Must be almost a foot long."

"Gopher tortoise?" Mama asked. "Never heard of it."

"Called that 'cause of the way he burrows. Digs a big, deep hole, jus' like a gopher. I reckon that burrow goes down eight feet or more. Keeps him safe and warm."

"Why was a rattlesnake down there, too?" I wanted to know.

"I was hopin' you'd ask, 'cause I jus' happen to have a story 'bout that. Want to hear it?"

"Yes," I said right away.

"How 'bout you, missuz?"

"Only if another snake doesn't come along."

"Then why don't you sit back down and rest a little more?"

Mama sat down and leaned against her tree.

"Once upon a time, near the dawn of the world, Mr. Rattlesnake was havin' a bad day. He'd made the mistake of showin' himself in Mr. Adam's garden. Mr. Adam done already had some trouble with a serpent once, and besides, he didn't like to see no poison snake near where his two boys was playin'. So Adam took out after that rattler, determined to chop off his head with his hoe. Mr. Rattlesnake saw him comin', and he knew he better find shelter or he was gon' be killed for sure.

"So off he slithered, jus' as fast as he could go. First he came to the rabbit family. 'Please let me crawl down your burrow,' he pleaded. 'Adam's after me, and he gon' chop off my head!' But the rabbits wouldn't let him in their burrow. They had a nest of new babies down there, and they was afraid that he would eat 'em all up.

"So Mr. Rattlesnake crawled on. Next he came to the groundhog and begged him for permission to hide in his hole. But the groundhog was afraid of the rattler's poison bite, so he told him no. Meanwhile, Mr. Adam was comin' closer and closer, holdin' that hoe like it was a sword.

"That rattler zipped along faster than ever until he came to the fox family, sittin' by their den in a hollow log," Bailey said. "'Please, friends,' he cried. 'Give me shelter or I'm gon' be killed for sure.' But the foxes wouldn't. They remembered how he had once swallowed one of their babies, and they were glad that now he about to pay for all his crimes."

I was enjoying Mr. Bailey's story. There was no Poppy to interrupt with a lot of questions, and I wasn't having to listen while ironing or doing some other chore at the same time. I looked at Mama leaning against the tree. Her eyes were closed, but she was smiling a little.

"Mr. Rattlesnake didn't know what to do. But jus' then he saw the gopher tortoise takin' the sun outside o' his burrow. Now, I forgot to tell you one very important thing about the gopher tortoise. In those long-ago days, he didn't have no shell. Anyway, the gopher tortoise saw the rattlesnake racin' toward him as fast as he could, shoutin' could he please crawl down his hole to save himself from Mr. Adam.

"Gopher tortoise could see he was gon' have to decide quick. That rattlesnake had never done nothin' to him or any of his kin, and he figured that he was a fellow critter, regardless of his bad reputation. In a lickety-split moment he decided and said to come on. That rattler shouted 'Thank you!' and zipped right by the tortoise, down into the hole. Then the tortoise saw Adam jus' a few steps away, brandishin' that hoe, and he decided *he'd* better get out o' the way, too. So down he crawled into the dark. Behind him, up in the daylight, he could hear Adam cussin' and carryin' on that Mr. Rattlesnake had got away from him.

"Now the snake was safe. He looked round and saw the tortoise huddled there in the corner. The gopher tortoise was plenty scared, but he politely welcomed Mr. Rattlesnake to his hole. Then that rascal snake said, 'I kind o' like it down here. It's downright comfortable. You's a much better digger than I am. Your deep hole will keep me safe, 'cause no man or animal can dig down this far to get me. With your kind permission, I think I'll stay.'"

Bailey stopped, took out his pipe and tobacco, and lit up. "Sho' is a beautiful afternoon," he said. "Ain't it, missuz?"

"Yes, it is," Mama agreed. "I'd be sound asleep by now if your story weren't so amusing. I want to hear what happens."

"It's almost done," Bailey said. "With that, Mr. Rattlesnake coiled himself up and went to sleep right there in the tortoise's parlor. Jus' before he put his head down, he yawned a ji-normous yawn so he could show off his long, needle-sharp fangs. He did that meanness on purpose, 'cause he knew that when Mr. Gopher Tortoise saw 'em, he'd be too scared ever to ask him to leave.

"Mr. Rattlesnake commenced to snore, and that kept the tortoise awake. Gave him a chance to think things over, too. He realized first off that he didn't really mind having Mr. Rattlesnake share his house, because he knew that no creature—Mr. Adam, neither—would come pokin' around long as they knew a poison snake was at home. But Mr. Gopher Tortoise was worried 'bout one thing: What if that rattler bit him by accident? Or what if Mr. Rattlesnake got hungry and decided to eat Mr. Gopher Tortoise and take that hole for himself?

"Then and there, that tortoise prayed to the Good Lord. 'O Lord, I'm willin' to have this here snake share my home, but I'm scared to death of his poison bite. Please help me.'

"The Lord heard that prayer. He decided he was gon' reward that tortoise for his kindness to a fellow critter. So when the tortoise woke up next morning, guess what had happened to him?"

"He had his shell," I said, pleased that I had figured it out a while earlier.

Bailey nodded his agreement. "The Lord gave the tortoise a shell to protect him from the terrible teeth of the rattlesnake. Now, whenever they need a new burrow, the tortoise digs it, 'cause he's got them big, strong claws. But he don't mind doin' the work, 'cause when Mr. Rattlesnake joins him in their parlor, he knows no one, man nor beast, is gon' mess with them. And that's why Mr. Rattlesnake and Mr. Gopher Tortoise live together.

"It seems to me this world is full o' folks who act jus' like Mr. Rattlesnake," Bailey added. "Ornery. Full o' poisonous words and deeds."

"Like Mrs. Davis and Mrs. Washington?" I asked. He nodded.

"I don't want to talk about them," Mama declared.

"We don't got to. Folks like that ain't my main point, anyway. What the story teaches is that it don't never hurt to show kindness. If we do, the Lord's gon' take care of us, jus' like he took care of Mr. Gopher Tortoise."

"So I have to be nice to the Miz Davises and Delia Washingtons of this world?" Mama asked. "After they mess me over?"

"I didn't say it's easy," Bailey replied. "I reckon we should be kind whenever we can, though. Don't you agree?"

Mama sighed. "I just wish other people knew that, too."

"You right about that," Bailey agreed. "But all we can do is decide for ourselves."

"Decide what?" I asked.

"If we're gon' live our lives actin' like Mr. Rattlesnake or Mr. Tortoise."

The following Friday I was sitting in the schoolyard, finishing my dinner. Miss Dolores had come by that morning to say that Poppy had a stomachache and wouldn't be going to school, so I was eating alone. Etta Mae and Jeralynn came and stood over me. Remembering Bailey's story, I said hello in the friendliest way I knew how.

"Bet I know somethin' *you* don't know," Jeralynn said.

I was determined to be nice. "I'm sure you know lots of things I don't. Different people know about different things."

"Not about things. About *someone*." She looked at me expectantly.

Had Etta Mae and Jeralynn changed their minds about me and decided to be friends at last? I was almost afraid to hope so, after the way they had treated me, but I was still willing to give them a chance. "Who is it about?" I asked.

"Somebody you know. Or *used* t' know." Etta Mae started to giggle, but Jeralynn looked at her and she stopped.

Something didn't feel right. "Who?" I repeated. I didn't know what else to say.

"Well," Jeralynn began slowly. "I heard Miz Delia Washington tellin' my mama all 'bout yo' daddy."

Now I was sure she was up to something. Mrs.

Washington wouldn't say anything good about anyone in our family. I stood up and looked Jeralynn in the eye, trying to act brave the way Mama had done in front of Mrs. Davis. "What about him? She shouldn't talk about my father. She doesn't know anything about him! He went away from here a long time ago."

"Maybe," Jeralynn said. "But some folks round here knows what happened to him."

"Why wouldn't they? He was in the war. He saved someone and got killed doing it. Daddy was a hero! I bet it was in the newspaper. That's why everybody knows about it."

"Your mama tell you that?" Jeralynn asked.

"Yes! It's the truth."

"That ain't what I heard Miz Delia say. She say your daddy . . . was a *bad* man. So bad, a policeman had to shoot him."

Jeralynn looked at Etta Mae, who nodded agreement.

My knees felt like they were giving way, but I stood as tall as I could. "That's not true. He was killed in the war."

"Miz Delia say your father a criminal. She say your mama lyin' to you about him bein' a hero." Jeralynn turned to Etta Mae. "Come on. Let's go."

They began to walk away. "Liars!" I shouted after them. "It's not true."

Jeralynn looked over her shoulder and sneered. "You'll find out," she declared.

I just stood there. "They're lying," I told myself. "I can prove it."

But how?

Time ran as slow as cold molasses that afternoon. I couldn't stop thinking about what Jeralynn said. Finally, I decided I'd just ask Mama. She'd assure me that Jeralynn was lying, that Daddy really had been killed in the war, and that he really was a hero. It was as easy as that.

Suddenly, Miss Johnson was asking me a question, and I couldn't answer. Of course everyone laughed, and Miss Johnson said, "Carissa, it's not like you to be daydreaming."

Walking home, I kept worrying over how to ask Mama my question. Mama didn't like talking about Daddy's death, but I had to ask her, anyway. Mrs. Washington and Jeralynn's mother were spreading lies, and I knew Mama wouldn't allow that. I had to tell her. She would want me to.

Then a new thought came into my head. What if Mama *had* been lying to me? She had always said that Daddy was killed in the war. But what if that wasn't true? Had something else happened to him, something too horrible to talk about? The idea made me feel sick to my stomach.

While waiting for Mama to get back from work, I planned what to say. But when she came through the door, I could see she'd been crying. "What's wrong, Mama?" I asked.

Mama dropped into the rocking chair. "I lost my job," she said wearily. "After dinner, the hotel owner told me he had to let me go. When I asked why, he couldn't give me a good reason. Just hemmed and hawed and said he was sorry. I can work next week, and that's it. At least the man gave me a week's notice."

"Mrs. Davis did it!" I cried.

"That's what I think, too. But there's no way to prove it. And even if we could, it wouldn't change a thing. We're at their mercy." Mama pushed herself to her feet. "I'm going to lie down. If I fall asleep, wake me in time to get some supper."

Mama patted me as she went by, and she closed herself in the bedroom.

There was no way to ask her about what Jeralynn had told me at school. Not now. If she learned that Mrs. Washington had been gossiping about us, she would run next door and get into the biggest fight yet. We didn't need that.

The weekend was miserable. Cold, drizzly weather didn't help. Mama still had to boil some laundry outdoors, rain or not, and we had to keep a good fire going in the fireplace and hang up clothes in front of it to get them dry. I asked if Poppy could come over, but Mama said she couldn't stand Poppy's chatter, so I ended up doing a big pile of ironing instead. My brain wouldn't give me any rest. Hundreds of times I relived the moment in the schoolyard when Jeralynn and Etta Mae had talked to me. I wished it had never happened. Why couldn't they have left me alone?

Monday morning finally arrived, just as cold and wet as the weekend had been. I got up, dressed, and ate breakfast, but I couldn't make my feet take me out the door. I couldn't face school—or Jeralynn and Etta Mae. Besides, who was there to make me go? Mama and Bailey had gone to work, and Granma, still hobbling around on a stiff ankle, would never walk down the muddy road to our house. So when Poppy arrived, I told her to go on—I was staying home.

She said she would keep me company.

I built up the fire in the fireplace. We wrapped ourselves in quilts and nestled in the rocking chairs. Of course, Poppy had to play with Zillah. That morning she changed her dress four times and rearranged her hair five. I read to Poppy from *The Thousand and One Nights* and shared my dinner with her. We kept telling each other what a fine time we were having, and how nice it was not to have to worry about mean girls like Jeralynn and Etta Mae, or the long walk to and from school.

When late afternoon came, Poppy went home. All of a sudden, I felt panicky, because soon I was going to have to lie to Mama and Bailey about my day.

To my surprise, lying came easily. I described events of a day at school that hadn't taken place. After supper, I studied my books and worked on assignments that Miss Johnson might have given.

Tuesday we stayed home again.

While Poppy played, I kept trying to figure out how to learn the truth about Daddy without having to ask Mama. Granma might know, but if I asked her, she would tell Mama. Jeralynn had said that Delia Washington knew about Daddy, but I would never in a million years ask our mean neighbor about my family's business.

We stayed home again on Wednesday, and Thursday, and Friday. Poppy acted as if it were a big adventure, but for me it wasn't. Each evening, Mama and Bailey asked about my day and accepted my lies. Each night, I lay in bed, hating myself for lying, hating Jeralynn for wrecking my life. Something terrible was going to happen, because sooner or later Mama would find out the truth. Then maybe she'd kill me and all my troubles would end.

On Saturday, just after dinner, we were cleaning house when Miss Johnson appeared at the door. My doom had come, but I felt relieved. Whatever was going to happen was going to happen *now*. I would be glad to have it over and done with.

"Good afternoon, Mrs. Hudson," Miss Johnson said. "Hello, Carissa."

"Hello," I managed to whisper.

"Miz Johnson, how are you?" said Mama. "Please come in the house."

"Just for a moment. I'm on my way to do some shopping." My teacher stepped inside.

"May I offer you a cup of tea?"

"No, thank you. I came by to find out if Carissa is feeling better."

This was it. Mama was about to know the truth, and I was about to receive the biggest punishment of my life. Strangely, I wasn't afraid. I was more curious to find out what would happen.

"'Feeling better'?" Mama looked at me. "She's feeling all right, as far as I know. Has she been sick at school?"

"No—she hasn't *been* to school all week. Neither has Poppy, so I assumed that they both were ill. I'm going to stop at the Tolivers' next and ask how Poppy is doing."

Mama took a quick step backward, as if someone had hit her. "'Hasn't been to school'? Of course she's been to school. Haven't you, Carissa?"

I hung my head. "No, ma'am."

Mama turned on me. "*What?* Where have you been, then?"

I stared at the floor.

Mama seized my chin and jerked my head up so that I had to look her in the eye. "If you haven't been to school, where *have* you been?"

"Here," I whispered.

"Here? All week long you told me you've been to school, and you've studied your lessons every night. How can you have been *here?*" She jerked my head up again. "Unless you've been lying to me."

Mama's eyes bored into mine. I wanted to look

away, but her hand clutched the sides of my chin, forcing me to face her. "How could you do such a thing?"

Still I said nothing.

"Answer me!" Mama demanded.

"Mrs. Hudson, I didn't mean to cause any trouble," Miss Johnson said in an anxious voice. "Perhaps I should go—"

"No, Miz Johnson. You've done me a big favor. This girl's evil had to be found out, and you've brought her sin to light. I thank you." Mama confronted me again. "I asked you a question. You've been lying, haven't you?"

"Yes, ma'am."

"Has Poppy been here with you all week?"

"Yes."

"That's the end of that! She's been a bad influence on you ever since the first day you knew her. I'm going to tell Dolores Toliver that her daughter can run wild, but not mine."

She let go of me, disgusted. "Miz Johnson, there's one thing I can promise you. This girl won't miss any more school unless I say she has to. If she does, you come tell me that very night. I won't let her throw away her only chance for some kind of real life by not going to school, so help me God."

"Mama—"

"Hush! I'll deal with you in a minute. Thank you, Miz Johnson, for coming over. I can handle this now."

Miss Johnson threw me a pitying glance. "I hope to see Carissa on Monday," she said.

"Oh, don't worry about that. She won't be missing any more school."

"I'm glad. Well, goodbye, Mrs. Hudson. Goodbye, Carissa."

Mama showed her to the door; then she advanced upon me. Her right arm rose, and I waited for the blow that would send me across the room. But when her hand was high above her head, Mama froze. Her hand fell, and she stumbled past me, collapsed into the rocking chair, and buried her face in her hands.

I stood bolted to the spot. But I *had* to explain, and that meant asking all the questions that had been torturing me for a week. I put my hand on her shoulder. "Mama . . ."

She shook me off. "Hush your mouth and get away from me! There's nothing you can say to explain away what you've done. Lord, what's going to become of us?" she wailed. "I'm working myself to death to provide for this ungrateful child, trying to keep body and soul together. And this is how she repays me. Making me play the fool in front of that teacher." Mama raised her head and glared at me. "It's going to be all over town by this evening that you can do as you please and I don't care any more about you than Dolores Toliver does about her little brat."

"Miss Johnson won't say anything to anyone. Besides, staying home from school was my idea, not Poppy's. I can explain! Won't you *please* listen to me?"

"Didn't I tell you to get out of my sight?" Mama

was crying now. "What have I ever done to anyone that all this is happening to me? I just can't take any more." She looked up and saw me still standing there, unable to speak or move. "I told you to get away from me!"

This time, I did. I ran out the back door. Mama slammed it behind me and turned the key in the lock.

FOURTEEN

❧

I walked around in the sunshine, trying to keep warm, but the cold air cut through my dress and sweater. The outhouse was warmer, but it smelled bad and I was terrified of the spiders. Finally, not knowing where else to go, I slipped into Bailey's shed.

It felt strange to be there. In all the months Bailey had been with us, he had never invited me inside. His few belongings were neatly arranged in the tiny room: an extra shirt and overalls hanging on pegs, a straw hat on the end of the bed, a kerosene lamp on a three-legged stool. I sat on the bed, and after a while I lay down and pulled the patchwork quilt up over my

head. The warm darkness underneath made me feel
safe.

❧

"Wake up, honey."

Rousing, I peeped from under the quilt into Bailey's
lined face, lit by the kerosene lamp in his hand.

"Wake up now. Supper's ready."

I sat up, pulling the quilt around my shoulders.
"What time is it?"

"Long after dark. About seven."

"How long have I been asleep?"

"I don't know. Come on. Your mama's got the food
on the table."

"I can't go in there. She locked me out."

"It's all right. Your mama's calmed down."

"She told you?"

"All about it. I come home, found you sleepin' here,
and went to ask why. She told me the whole story."

"Is she still mad?"

"I reckon not. She's not too happy with you,
though. You're gon' have to go some to earn back her
trust. No more missin' school." Bailey looked down at
me kindly. "Why'd you do it, honey?"

I wished Mama had been able to ask me that.
"Jeralynn told me something bad about my daddy last
week, and I didn't want to go back to school anymore."

Bailey sat down next to me and put the lantern on
the little stool. "What'd she say?"

"She said Mrs. Washington told her mama that Daddy was shot by a policeman."

"I thought he was killed in the war."

"Jeralynn said Daddy was a bad man—a criminal—and the police had to shoot him."

Bailey sighed. He put his arm around me and held me close. "There's one way to find out the truth."

"Ask Mama?"

"Uh-huh."

"I'm afraid to."

"I figured that. Otherwise, you'd'a asked her days ago and spared yourself all this grief. You ready to ask her now?"

I said I was, and we went to the cabin.

Mama was standing at the stove. She eyed me sternly but said nothing.

"Missuz, could we sit for a moment and talk before we eat?" Bailey asked. "Carissa got somethin' to say to you."

"Yes, she does," Mama declared. "Like an apology."

"That, too," Bailey agreed. "Could we all sit down?"

We pulled up chairs next to the fire.

"Go on, Carissa," Bailey prompted me. "Tell us what happened."

As soon as my words were out, Mama fell back in the chair and moaned, in a choked voice, "O my Lord. My Lord!"

"Mama!" I started to get up.

Bailey held me back. "Jus' let her be for a minute."

Mama called on God and the Lord Jesus for help. She buried her face in her hands and started to cry.

"Can you tell us about it, missuz?" Bailey asked after a while. "What really happened to your husband?"

Mama pushed herself up, her eyes blazing. "I swear to God I'm going to kill Delia Washington for spreading a lie about Raymond. Doesn't *anybody* in this town have an ounce of pity? This is the last straw! We're going to get out of here if I have to rob the bank and walk over every living soul, black or white, to do it."

"What happened, Mama?" I asked.

She sighed. "I'll tell you the truth. I should have told you before, just as soon as you were old enough to understand. I thought I could protect you, but I've been a fool about that, like so many other things."

I felt like I couldn't get enough air. Maybe outside, I could breathe. I had to go there, catch my breath. But I had to know why Mama had lied to me. I stayed where I was.

"Sugar, your daddy didn't die in Europe. He was killed by a policeman on a Philadelphia street three days after he stepped off of the ship from fighting the war in France."

So Jeralynn *hadn't* been lying. But I didn't want to accept it. "No, Mama!" I cried. "That can't be true!"

"I'm afraid it is," Mama said quietly.

I was trying to make sense of things, but I couldn't. Maybe Mama had lied to me about other things. Lots of things. No, that was impossible. "How did Daddy get shot?" I asked at last.

"He had just come home. It was the happiest day of my life when I saw him come through the door of our apartment. He looked so good in that uniform! I hadn't seen him in more than a year, but he was the same Raymond. None of the awful stuff he'd had to do overseas had changed him. I could tell that. His soul was still just as good and kind as ever.

"For two days, he didn't leave the apartment. He just kept holding me in his arms and holding you and playing with you, Carissa. You were afraid of him at first—he was a stranger to you—but by that second day, you were laughing and going right to his arms. You *knew* he was your daddy; that's for sure.

"Then on the third day he wanted to go out into the neighborhood and see some of his old friends. He put his uniform on because he was so proud of it. He kissed me and told me how he'd kept himself alive in the war so he could come home to us. Then he picked you up and tossed you to get you to laugh. He went out the door—and that was the last time I ever saw him alive."

I wanted to crawl into Mama's lap. "What happened?" I whispered.

"He got shot trying to help a white woman who was being beaten by a white policeman. He was just walking along the sidewalk, minding his own business, when he came across the policeman clubbing the woman with his nightstick. Folks who saw it happen said that the woman went down, but the cop kept hitting her. She was screaming and trying to defend herself. And they said she was bleeding from her head. Raymond went to that woman's defense because nobody else would. He tried to stop the policeman and they got to scuffling, and the cop punched at Raymond and Raymond hit him back. Then the cop pulled his gun and shot your daddy square in the chest. The bullet went right through his heart, and he dropped down dead.

"He fought his way through France and came home safe and sound to us only to be laid low by Sergeant Arthur White, an *officer of the law*."

"What happened to that policeman?" Bailey asked. "I reckon he went to trial."

Mama nodded tiredly. "He went to trial . . . and the jury found him not guilty in fifteen minutes. They said that he was justified in shooting Raymond because he was acting in self-defense."

Mama beckoned me to her and put her arms around me. "I know I should have told you, but it seemed like too much to put on your shoulders. And now you had to hear it from a stranger when you should have heard it from your own mama.

"That white woman was nothing to him," she told Bailey. "I've wished a thousand times that he had left that mess alone. Why did my Raymond have to get involved? Didn't Carissa and I need him more than some stranger on a city street? People ought to mind their business and let folks handle their own messes! There's one thing I've learned: When you try to help someone, you're going to end up sorry you did."

Bailey just sat rocking slowly. Mama held me while the fire on the hearth died down to a bed of softly glowing orange coals. On the table our dinner of beans, greens, and corn bread got cold.

❧

Next morning after breakfast, Mama apologized again for not telling me the truth in the first place. Then she wanted to discuss something else: my return to school.

"No! I can't ever go back there."

"I understand how you feel, sugar. Do you think I want to face the people of this town, knowing some of them are still talking about your daddy's death? Do you think I *want* to let our kind neighbor know just what I think of her? I don't. But I can't let it pass. She knew what she said would get back to you through that little witch Jeralynn. I'm going to to face her, let her know she can't wipe her feet all over us like we were her doormat. And you have to face the children at school."

"I can't go back and tell why I stayed home."

"I've been thinking of how to deal with this thing. First, I'll write to Miz Johnson. We owe her an explanation, and I don't want her thinking bad about you."

"What do I say when the others ask me where I was?"

"Tell them you didn't feel like going to school, so you stayed home. That's all you need to say. Let *them* deal with it. They'll think what they want, anyway. So tell the truth—just not all of it."

"But what if Jeralynn tells everyone that a policeman killed Daddy for being a bad man?"

"*Then* you have a powerful weapon to fight her lies."

"What?"

"The truth. You just have to be brave enough to tell it."

"I wanted to tell you what Jeralynn said about Daddy. But that was the day you got fired. You looked so sad that I didn't want to say anything."

"You were trying to protect *me* from more hurt. That was so thoughtful."

"After I played hooky, I was afraid to tell you."

"And it got harder and harder to say anything?"

I nodded.

"I hope we've both learned a lesson," Mama said. "You know what it is, don't you?"

"Telling the truth is better," I said.

"Even when it hurts," Mama added.

I still didn't want to go back, but Mama insisted. She said each day away would make it harder to return.

The next morning, Mama made sure I was up before she went to work. I told her my stomach ached, and it did. She said she believed me but that it made no difference. She saw to it that my dinner was made and that I was fully dressed before she left the house. Then Bailey knocked at the back door and offered to walk me to school. That made it a little easier.

Poppy appeared just as we were ready to leave. Mama had talked to Miss Dolores and gotten things straightened out, so Poppy and I were still allowed to be friends. But Mama also said that if we messed up even one more time, she would never let us see each other again. We promised to be good.

Having Poppy as an ally helped, but my breakfast of grits and bread still felt like bricks in my stomach as I said goodbye to Bailey in the schoolyard. Now I really felt sick.

Miss Johnson took the letter of explanation Mama had written, read it, nodded to me, and called us to order. The morning went as usual. Nothing happened until dinnertime, when Etta Mae and Jeralynn cornered me and Etta Mae asked if I'd missed school to work at the hotel with my mama before her job gave out. They knew Mama had lost her job, too! My heart was jumping in my chest. "Run away," I told myself. "Go get Miss Johnson."

There she was, watching some boys play baseball. I took a step in her direction.

"Gon' run to the teacher, little baby?" Jeralynn taunted.

She had gone too far. Finally, I'd had enough of being pushed around. I planted my feet and looked her in the eye.

"So did yuh have t' help yo' mama cook?" Etta Mae asked again.

"No," I said. Poppy came up next to me.

"Then yuh musta been sick," asserted Jeralynn.

"No," I replied.

"What yuh mean?"

"I just didn't come to school, that's all. Poppy and I stayed home, at my house."

There. It was out.

"Yuh jus' stayed home for no reason?" I could tell she didn't believe me.

"We didn't feel like going to school, and we didn't."

"You and Poppy both?"

"Yes."

"What you gon' do 'bout it?" Poppy challenged. "Ain't no business of yours what Carissa and me do. Why don't you go pick your nose?"

Jeralynn ignored her. "Your mama knew yuh did that?"

"No."

"Her mama know?"

"No," Poppy declared. "What you care?"

"What did you do all day?" Etta Mae asked.

"None of your business."

"Oooh, I bet yo' mama whupped yo' butt when she found out."

"She did not," I said. "She didn't touch me."

"She not whup yuh?" Jeralynn said, wonder in her voice.

"You deaf?" Poppy asked her. "She *said* she didn't get whupped."

"She just talked to me," I told them.

"That all? Fo' true?" Etta Mae marveled.

"That's all."

Jeralynn looked at me as though I were either crazy or the biggest liar she had ever met.

I looked back. "Any more questions? Poppy and I are busy."

We walked away, but over my shoulder I saw them go directly to a group of girls jumping rope. The jumping ceased, and then the whispering began. They all looked in our direction.

"It's starting," I said to myself. "Before we go back into the building for the afternoon, every single boy and girl will know what we did. The teasing, the whispering, and the pointing will never, ever, *ever* stop."

But to my surprise, it never started. Instead of being teased, I won a kind of respect that day. No longer was I the girl who always knew her lessons and never talked out of turn in class. I became the mystery girl who had dared to skip an *entire week* of school without anyone knowing. I was a girl who could be naughty. Who could tell what I might do next?

Walking home that day, I thought about what had happened. Telling the truth had scared me, but it made things better, just as Mama had said it would. Now, if Jeralynn said anything to anyone about how Daddy had died, I could tell the truth about him and feel good about doing it.

When I told Mama that evening, she patted me and

said she was proud of me. When I asked why, she said it was because I was brave—braver than she was.

"There's just one thing I pray now," Mama added.

"What?"

"That knowing about what really happened to your daddy won't make you think less of him. I know how important it was to you to believe he was a war hero."

"Nobody made him help that lady. He decided to do that all by himself. Doesn't that make him a hero?"

"Yes, it does. That makes him a *real* hero. Don't ever forget it."

"Mama—"

"Sugar?"

"Don't you forget it, either."

Fifteen

Friday morning at school, I was studying my spelling words when I felt a tap on my shoulder. I turned, and Dorothy Hawkins, who sat in back of me, whispered, "I got a note for you. Put your hand down." I looked to see if Miss Johnson was watching, but she was helping some of the younger children with their arithmetic. Slowly, I dropped my hand to my side and felt Dorothy press a folded piece of paper into it.

No one had *ever* passed me a note in school. I guess the other children thought I was too serious or too much of a teacher's pet to be interested in such things. The other students passed notes all the time, and sometimes Miss Johnson caught them. When she did, she read the note out loud.

Who would be sending me a note? I felt my heart beat fast. I unfolded it and read, "Want to jump rope at recess? Daisy." I glanced to where Daisy McCoy was sitting. She was watching me. I smiled at her and nodded, and she smiled back.

For a second, I wondered if Jeralynn had made Daisy write to me. Maybe Jeralynn was hoping I'd get caught with the note and be embarrassed when Miss Johnson read it to the class. Maybe the other girls wouldn't let me jump rope, after all. But I knew that Daisy wasn't friends with Jeralynn or Etta Mae and probably wouldn't do them any favors.

On the playground, Daisy came over to where Poppy and I were eating. Daisy invited both of us to eat with her and some of the other girls. We did, and then we all jumped rope.

From that day on, my classmates, except for Etta Mae and Jeralynn, started to notice me more. I sometimes got notes, had people whisper secrets to me and make me promise not to tell, and was included in the jump-rope games, which Etta Mae and Jeralynn wouldn't play. They said jump rope was for babies. I didn't care. It was fun.

At home, things were better, too. Mama talked about Daddy sometimes. One evening, Granma sat with us and told us stories about when Daddy was young. I had never heard how good he was at baseball, or how he had once caught a twelve-pound bass from Durden's Pond. Granma said she had the hardest time getting Daddy to let her cook it. He wanted to show that bass all up and down Canoochee Road, and by the time he did give it to her, it was already starting to smell.

Mama told me how she'd met Daddy in the store where she was working, and how funny his southern accent had sounded to her. She said he was a real gentleman with perfect manners, no matter how strangely he talked.

Listening to Mama and Granma made me feel closer to Daddy than I ever had. Before, he had been a soldier in a uniform, whose picture sat on our dresser. Now he was becoming real. Daddy had lived on Canoochee Road and done the same things I was doing now. Maybe he'd caught crawfish in the creek and picked up pecans. Maybe he'd watched for rattlesnakes and gopher tortoises to come up out of their holes.

Mama was also feeling happier because she had gotten another job, a better one than she had at the hotel. Some new people had come to Summit, white folks from Atlanta, and they had opened a boarding house. They needed someone to manage the kitchen, and they hired Mama. She had two girls working under her direction, so she didn't have to do all the cooking or any of the cleanup herself. Mama liked the work and said that the people she worked for were "clean, fair, and honest." Now when she came home in the evening, she was tired from working hard, but not angry and exhausted.

We kept on with our laundry business, but we still didn't have as many customers as we had before Mrs. Davis caused trouble. Mama said it was okay, because she was making pretty good money at the boarding house and we didn't need to do as much wash. I was glad for that. I had come to hate the sight of the boiling pot, and the thought of ironing piles of clothes made me shudder.

But then Bailey started acting strange. He didn't say much in the evenings, and sometimes he looked unhappy. One Saturday evening, he didn't come home from work, and he was gone all day Sunday. Mama fretted about him, but this time she didn't say anything about how he might be drinking or getting into trouble. I figured she knew by now that Bailey wouldn't do those things.

"Come into the house," Mama said when he knocked on the door just at suppertime on Sunday. "I got some fresh coffee on the stove, and the food will be done in a little while. I'm so glad to see you, Mr. Bailey. Carissa and I have been worried."

Bailey sat and took the coffee. "Thank you," he said. "This sho' tastes good." He was quiet for a moment, staring at the mug.

"What is it?" Mama asked him. "Something troubling you?"

"I been wantin' to explain somethin' to both o' you

for quite some time," Bailey answered, "but I didn't know how to start. It's been eatin' at me bad, and I owe you an explanation about where I been all weekend. I ain't proud o' part of the story I got to tell you, but it's better if the truth comes out. You taught me that, missuz."

I sat down at the table, and Mama took the other rocker. I couldn't imagine what it was Bailey had to tell us, but it had to be something serious. A familiar feeling came over me, the same feeling I had had when Jeralynn and Etta Mae told me about Daddy. Part of me didn't want to hear what Bailey had to say, but another part did. I was all quivery inside.

"Whatever it is, you can tell us," Mama said. "Don't you know you're part of this family?"

It pleased me to hear Mama say that. For a long time, I'd hoped and prayed she would come to love Bailey, too.

"Bless you for that," Bailey said. "I been feelin' like I belong here with you and Carissa, and I hoped y'all felt the same. Truth is, you two, and Miz Rachel, been the only family I've had for many a year. I can't begin to say what it means to me, bein' able to live here with you."

"What do you want to tell us?" Mama asked gently.

"This'll take a little time. And I got to begin with an apology, 'cause somethin' I told you and Carissa months ago ain't quite the exact truth."

What might not have been true? I couldn't imagine. I hoped it wasn't going to be something bad; then I felt angry at myself for even thinking such a thing. Bailey *couldn't* do anything wrong.

"Go on," Mama said.

"Do you remember what I told you last fall about losin' my wife and daughter over in Alabama, a long time ago?"

"Yes, you said they died of the fever."

"That's what I said. And that's partly true. But it warn't in Alabama. It was right near here, down by Stillmore."

"Stillmore!" Mama exclaimed. "That's just a few miles away. You lived near *here?*"

"Yes, ma'am. I *was* born in west Georgia, like I told you, over near Albany, and after runnin' away from sharecropping, when I couldn't stand it no more, I wandered around the state, findin' work. Finally ended up near here. Railroad was pretty new then, and they were cuttin' lots o' pine and shippin' it south. I found me a job at the mill, and went and got Hannah and Serena over from where I'd left 'em, over in west Georgia, near Cordele. That was a long trip, but I had to have them with me.

"We got a place in a little village o' colored folks near Stillmore. I worked at the mill during the day, and in the evenin's did carpentry work, helpin' other families build little places. Worked for some white folks nearby as well as colored. Hannah did what she could,

too: kept chickens, raised a garden, did some cookin'
and cleanin' for white ladies."

I sat perfectly still, fascinated. He had told us so
much about himself already that I had never stopped
to think there might be a lot more he hadn't said. When
we first met Bailey, Mama had told me we didn't know
who he was, not really. I was starting to understand
what she meant.

"All that happened right near here," Mama said.
"Imagine that! I never would have thought."

"Everything was goin' good," Bailey continued.
"We had our own little community, a church, a store
where the men could sit on the porch and pass the
time. Those was the happiest two years o' my life.
That's how long it lasted, two years.

"When Hannah and Serena came down with the
fever, it scared everyone. Then others got it, too—lots of
'em. Folks were frightened to death they'd catch it, so
they hesitated to come into a house where the fever had
struck. Besides, most families had they own sick to look
after. I nursed Hannah and Serena best I could, but they
needed care all day and all night. Soon I couldn't go on
by myself, 'cause I hadn't had no sleep in five days.

"The sixth day, someone knocked on the door. I
opened it and there stood a strange woman. A *white*
woman. 'I'm here to help you,' she said. And in she
came. I didn't say no. At that point, I didn't care who
it was—black, white, or red. Her name was Eliza
Whitaker. She lived with her husband and children on

a farm five miles away. Told me she'd heard about our trouble and knew it was her Christian duty to come help us in our time of need. She took over right away and sent me to bed myself. That lady was the best nurse I've ever seen. My Hannah died in her arms. Then Mr. Whitaker come and helped me dig the grave. They was merciful to me and mine when no one else would help. That's why I can't ever say that all white folks is bad," he said slowly. Bailey looked right at Mama when he said it, like he wanted to be sure she understood.

My eyes were brimming with tears. I wanted to say something, but no words would come.

"I'm so sorry," Mama said. "I had no idea."

"You told us your wife *and* little girl died," I said.

"I said that because I couldn't stand to tell you the truth. Serena didn't die. She pulled through, and life went on. But that little house where Hannah and I had been so happy started to feel like a prison. I knew I had to go find work somewhere else. But I couldn't take a five-year-old child with me. I asked my neighbors, Hiram and Louisa Tanner, if they would keep Serena for a while, look after her till I found a job and came back to get her. They said they would, and I gave 'em some money to help pay for anything she would need. Then I took off. Finally found another good job back where I come from. But when I went back to Stillmore, the Tanners was gone, and so was Serena."

"What?" Mama cried. "They stole your daughter?"

I couldn't stand to hear any more. I started to get up, but then I dropped back into my seat. There was no way to run away from the truth.

"No, missuz. I don't believe it was like that. While I was gone, the fever struck again, and a lot o' folks ran away. They was jus' plain scared. The Tanners left word for me: they was headin' toward the coast, toward Savannah, where Hiram was from, and said I should come on and find 'em with their people in Thunderbolt. I took off right away. But when I got over to Thunderbolt and found some Tanners, they didn't know nothin' about Hiram and Louisa. Hadn't seen 'em or heard from 'em in a long time.

"I didn't know what to do, so I settled down to wait. But the days passed, and turned into weeks, and they was no word. Nothin'. I got a job—had to—needed a way to live, and had to have somethin' to keep me from thinkin' 'bout my troubles. As it was, I pretty near lost my mind, anyway.

"Finally, I had to hit the road and find Serena myself. And that's what I did. I've been all over, lookin' for my daughter, these past thirty years. Every so often I'd have somebody write to the folks I'd gotten to know in Thunderbolt, to see if any word ever come from the Tanners. None ever did."

A look of grief so strong crossed Bailey's face that I thought he would start sobbing, but he held himself together. I had never felt as sorry for anyone as I felt for Bailey at that moment.

"How did you happen to come back by here?" Mama asked him.

"That day last September, when I stopped in front of this house, I was headed to Stillmore. I hadn't been there in years, but I kept feelin' myself drawn down there, to see the place where Hannah is buried. I wanted to tell her that I been lookin' for our Serena, lookin' everywhere. And I wanted to tell her I was sorry—for ever lettin' Serena go in the first place."

Bailey pulled out his handkerchief and wiped his eyes. "When I met Carissa and you that day, I realized how tired I was of searchin'. You offered me some supper, and when I got down the road that night, I thought to myself, 'Go on back. Maybe you can still have you a family.' And when I came back and y'all were so kind to me, I started pretendin' that you was Serena, all growed up, and Carissa was my little granddaughter.

"Then I knew I had to visit Hannah down in Stillmore. So I went down there, that first time I was gone for the weekend, and found the place where Mr. Whitaker and I buried her. Other colored folks had been buried there, too. My Hannah didn't have no marker, so I ordered one for her. That's what I did the second time I visited. And this weekend, the marker was done and the man from the company put it over Hannah's grave. That's where I been."

I left my chair and went to Bailey and climbed into his lap as if I were a child. His arms felt strong around me, and I laid my head on his chest. The rough cloth of his coat smelled of his sweet pipe tobacco.

"I'm sorry I wasn't brave enough to tell y'all the truth from the start," Bailey said. He started patting my back. "I'm so ashamed of myself for ever lettin' Serena go. A child needs her daddy. I've tortured myself a thousand times wonderin' what she thought when I left her and never came back. She was only five! How could she understand? I never should of left her. And I been payin' for it ever since."

"Come back by me," Mama told me. "Let Mr. Bailey be for a minute."

I got up and went to my place.

Bailey reached for his pipe, changed his mind, and put it back into his coat pocket. "I hoped that puttin' that marker on Hannah would bring me some peace, and it has—a little. But somewhere out there is my Serena, not knowin' why her daddy ran off and left her. Part of me says I got to hit the road again, keep searchin' till I find her, even if it takes till my dyin' day. Then at least I could stand before the Lord and tell him that I never stopped tryin'. Another part of me jus' wants to stay here forever, with you and Carissa."

Happiness washed over me. Bailey *had* to stay. After thirty years, he could never find Serena. The country was too big, and he didn't know where to look. "Please stay with us," I said. "Mama is right. You belong to our family now."

"That's jus' how I feel, sugar," he said. "I even

thought for a while about seein' if maybe Miz Rachel and I could get to like one another well enough to marry. Then I could of moved in with her and made it all official. But Miz Rachel is set in her ways, and she got her strong opinions 'bout things, and I come to realize that we'd only make each other miserable if we was to get married."

I remembered the evening Granma had gotten herself all fixed up with makeup and perfume. I couldn't imagine the two of them together then, and I couldn't now. Besides, Bailey belonged to us . . . But somehow, that idea didn't feel quite right, either.

Mama laughed. "I agree you're better off just being Miz Rachel's friend."

A tiny smile crossed Bailey's face. "Missuz, I've got to ask you and Carissa what to do. I feel like a lost child."

"I don't think we can tell you that," Mama replied. "But there is one thing I want to say. I've come to be mighty fond of you, and Carissa loves you like you were her own granddaddy. As far as we're concerned, you can stay with us as long as you want. Forever, if it suits you."

"Please stay," I begged.

"Bless you both," Bailey said. "Those is the sweetest words I've heard since I lost Hannah and Serena."

It was settled, then; everything had turned out just as I had hoped. I had new friends at school, Mama had a good job, and Bailey was going to stay. In just a few moments, all my sadness for Bailey's losses had turned to happiness. I looked at Bailey expectantly, waiting for him to agree.

Then I noticed something behind Bailey's kind face: Daddy's picture sitting on the pine dresser. From his photograph, Daddy smiled at me as he always did. He looked so young and handsome in his army uniform! A question began to form in the back of my mind. I knew what it was, and I didn't want to pay it any attention. I shook my head, trying to make it go away. It wouldn't. Instead, the question got bigger and bigger until I almost thought I could see it written in large letters right in front of me.

If Daddy had lost me when I was a little girl, would he have kept looking for me until he found me, no matter how long it took?

I knew he would. That was the kind of man Daddy was. He had died trying to help a stranger, so surely he would have spent all his life trying to find me, because he would have known that I needed him. Daddy had put a strange woman before himself. I was his daughter, and he would want me to do the same for Bailey.

I ached deep inside, but now I knew what was right. "You have to find Serena," I told Bailey.

"Why, Carissa!" Mama cried.

"You have to try again," I said.

Bailey tilted his head a little and looked into my eyes. "Why is that, honey?"

"She needs you. I wish *my* daddy could come back.

He can't, but if he could, it would be the best thing that ever happened. You have to try."

"But then I'd have to leave you. I hate even thinkin' about it."

"So do I! I wanted you to stay and be like my daddy. But that was selfish of me."

"No, it warn't," Bailey said.

"Of course it wasn't," Mama agreed.

"Maybe it wasn't before I knew about Serena," I went on. "She's out there somewhere, Mr. Bailey, still wondering about you—just like you said. If you were *my* daddy, I'd want you to find me, no matter how long it took. So does she! You have to try one more time."

I stopped, embarrassed at myself for saying so much. Bailey closed his eyes for a minute, then opened them again and looked at me. I noticed Mama was staring at me, too.

"You can come back one day," I said to Bailey, searching for a way to make things better. "After you find Serena. She can come with you."

"Of course I can," he said. "I'll see y'all again. Serena'll come with me. You jus' wait and see."

"We'll make sure of it, won't we?" Mama added.

"Come here, Carissa," Bailey said.

I went and stood in front of him. He took both of my hands in his and looked at me tenderly. "I've never known anyone more loving than you," he said. "Or braver, or less selfish. No matter what ever happens, you're always gon' be my little girl."

Two days later, we stood in our yard as Bailey tied his bedroll onto the back fender of the blue bicycle and strapped on his pack. Granma and Poppy had come to help see him off. When all his belongings were stowed, there was nothing to do except the one thing that all of us dreaded. Poppy jumped into Bailey's arms and held on for dear life. After Mama pried her off, Bailey took Granma aside for a moment and whispered something into her ear. She nodded, then kissed him on the cheek.

Then Mama took Bailey by both hands. "You be careful. Let us hear from you. And when you find Serena, bring her for a visit. No matter what happens, you always have a home with us."

Bailey put his arms around her and held her as if she were his own daughter.

I watched, waiting for my tears to come, but my eyes were dry. I didn't want the last thing Bailey saw to be me crying. Besides, I wasn't feeling sad, exactly. I felt happy, in a strange way—happy that Bailey was going to find Serena. He would, this time. I felt sure of it.

He put his arm around me. "You way too big to pick up," he said. "I know I can trust you to help your mama. Be good to her, hear? She's a treasure."

How grown up I felt at that moment!

He leaned down to whisper in my ear. "Your mama's gon' be all right, now. And so are you."

"I love you so much," I said. "I always have."

"I know, honey. Me, too."

Bailey climbed onto the bicycle and started off. He waved at us, then headed down the open road. He got smaller and smaller, and finally disappeared around the sharp bend in Canoochee Road.

It was still before dinnertime on a Tuesday, and Mama had to get to work. She sent Poppy to school. I didn't have to go—just this once—because Mama didn't think I'd be able to pay attention to my lessons; Miss Johnson would understand. Mama left for work, and Granma and I stood in the road, as if we couldn't think of what to do next. It felt strange that things looked just the same but everything was different. Granma went inside to prepare dinner. I offered to help, but she said she could manage by herself.

I was left in the road alone. This was where Bailey had taught me how to ride his bicycle. He had promised me that someday I would have my own bike, but that seemed impossible now. When would I ever get the chance to ride again?

I walked around the side of the cabin and went into Bailey's shed. Inside, things were in perfect order. The patchwork quilt was spread neatly on the bed; the kerosene lantern stood on the little stool next to it. The small, plain room seemed ready for Bailey to come back at any moment.

Granma called me for dinner, but I couldn't eat. Instead, I started sobbing and let her put me to bed, where I cried myself into a dreamless sleep.

The sound of knocking woke me. When Mama answered the door, I realized she was home from work, and it was late afternoon. Who was at the door?

Bailey! It had to be him. He'd changed his mind and come back!

I jumped up and hurried to the front room to welcome him home. But it wasn't Bailey. Mama was at the door, talking to a white boy. He handed her an envelope and said that "an old colored man" had paid him a dime to deliver it. Mama thanked him, and the boy went on his way.

"What is it?" I asked.

"Good afternoon to you, too," Mama teased. "I'm glad to see you. Granma went home just a little while ago. She told me about putting you to bed. She's mighty broken up over Bailey, too." She hugged me. "How are you feeling, sugar?"

"Awful. When I heard the knocking I thought for a minute—" I couldn't say any more.

"That it was Bailey?"

I nodded.

"That's all right. So did I."

"You did?" Somehow knowing that Mama had shared my hope made me feel better.

"Yes, indeed. It just doesn't seem possible that he's gone. Getting used to it is going to take some time—for both of us. Let's see what this is."

Inside the envelope was a folded piece of paper with writing on it, and inside that was a tidy pile of money.

"What in the world?" Mama gasped.

"Bailey sent us all that? Why?"

"I don't know."

I couldn't take my eyes off the money. It was more than I'd ever seen in one place before. How could it possibly be for us? "The letter," I said. "What does it say?"

Mama started reading. "It *is* for us. There's enough money to help us get away from here. It's enough for two tickets back to Philadelphia, with some extra to help us get settled."

"Oh, Mama!"

"That Bailey . . . That Bailey."

"Read what it says."

Her voice trembled. "Dear Missuz and Carissa, I am having a white lady I know write this for me. She promised that her son would deliver it. This money is for you to use to go back to Philadelphia. I have checked the price of the tickets and I know it is enough. When the time is right, I pray you will be able to go there and be happy.

"Carissa, I have something for you, too. You'll find it by the gopher tortoise hole. Don't be sad that I am gone. Remember all our good times. Study hard in school and remember all that you have learned. I love you and I pray that God will watch over you and bless you forever. Never forget to be kind. I will write and let you know about what I find. Goodbye, missuz, and goodbye, Carissa. Love, Bailey."

Mama kept saying, "That Bailey . . . That Bailey."

"Can I go and see what he left me?"

"You want me to come with you?"

"No, ma'am. I think I want to go alone."

"Go on, then, and come right back when you're done."

It seemed like a long walk out to the sand hills. Lonely, too. When I got to the gopher tortoise burrow, I found something I recognized—Mr. Bailey's leather pouch, hanging on a branch of an oak tree. Inside it were the sand dollar and a note. I sat down on a bare spot and held the sand dollar, turning it over to examine both sides in the golden sunshine of late afternoon. Yes, there were the flower petals and the tiny, perfect star on the rounded top; on the bottom were the veined shapes of leaves.

The message was written by the same hand that had taken down the letter Bailey had sent to Mama: *When the time is right, let the birds go free. Bailey.*

I shook the sand dollar. It rattled. The birds were inside, ready to fly.

"When the time is right," the note said. It was up to me. Bailey had made me promise to go to the ocean. When I did, I would find another sand dollar. Hundreds of sand dollars. A thousand.

I snapped the sand dollar in half. Two miniature white birds fell into my lap. I broke the halves, and there were two more. Another break and there was the fifth tiny bird. I put them into the pouch, and then I buried the pieces of the sand dollar in the soft earth near the mouth of the burrow.

I thought perhaps I should feel sad, but I didn't.

Instead, I felt like running, and I did, almost all the way home.

As I came to our cabin, I knew what I wanted to do next. I burst through the door and asked, "May I go to Poppy's?"

"I suppose, but tell me first what Bailey left for you. Not his bicycle, I hope. He needs that."

"No, ma'am, his pouch with the sand dollar in it."

"Oh, that was thoughtful. Something to remember him by."

I didn't want to take the time to explain that I'd broken the sand dollar and buried the pieces. I could tell Mama about that later. She would understand. "May I go to Poppy's?" I asked again.

"Yes, go. But it's nearly time for supper, so don't be too long."

I ran to Poppy's and asked Miss Dolores if Poppy could come out for a while.

She said yes, then told me how sorry she was Bailey was gone and said we must all be pretty broken up about it. I assured her we were.

As we reached our cabin, I said to Poppy, "Let's climb the magnolia tree."

"For real?"

"Yes. Come on."

I couldn't go up the tree as fast as Poppy, but she waited for me and showed me where to put my feet. "Don't look down," she advised.

She didn't have to tell me that.

Quicker than I would have thought possible, we were high in the tree. I climbed even farther up than Poppy did and stood on a sturdy branch, holding on to the main trunk and looking out over the road. Poppy was on another branch.

"Look for Bailey," Poppy suggested.

"He's gone too far by now."

"Which way was he goin'?"

"I don't know. Maybe to Savannah."

"Which way is that?"

I pointed east, where the sky was darkening in the twilight. "Show me Swainsboro," I said.

"I can't."

"Why not? You said you could see Swainsboro and Atlanta from up here."

Poppy grinned. "I was makin' a joke."

"I know. You can't really see that far."

Off to the north, a sea of pine trees faded into purple gloom. But it seemed to me that I *could* see far, far across the miles, all the way to the bright city of Philadelphia.

❧

Mama cooked my favorite hot cakes for supper and let me have a mug of sweet tea. After the dishes were washed up, we made a little fire on the hearth even though the room was warm. We wanted the comforting glow of the coals.

I got Zillah from her shelf and held her in my lap while Mama took up some mending. "Where do you think Mr. Bailey is by now?" I asked.

"Lord only knows. Somewhere bedded down for the night."

"How does he know where to look for Serena?"

"I'm not sure. I guess wherever his heart tells him to go."

"I'm worried about him."

"No need for that. Mr. Bailey can take care of himself."

We talked about him, laughed, cried a little more, and went to bed early. I'd slept half the afternoon, but I was more tired than I could ever remember being.

When we were tucked in, I asked Mama something I'd been thinking of all evening. "When are we going home?"

"What do you mean?"

"To Philadelphia. We have the money. We can go as soon as we want."

"It's not that easy, sugar."

"Why not? Don't you want to go?"

"Of course I do. A few months ago, I'd have taken Bailey's money and been on the next train. But we can't just leave your granma. She doesn't have anyone else but us now. What will she do after we're gone?"

"She can come with us."

"Maybe . . . And we *will* go. I just don't know when."

"When the time is right," I said.

"Yes," Mama agreed. "When the time is right."

Sixteen

❧

New York City, October 1929

The subway train roared along in the dark tunnel, bound for Coney Island and the Atlantic Ocean. "When will we be there?" I asked.

"How should I know?" Mama replied. "I've never been here before."

I couldn't sit still. There was nothing to see in the tunnel, and I was eager to be back in the open air. Besides, underneath my dress I was wearing an itchy bathing suit. I wanted to scratch myself in ten places at once, but Mama said it wasn't ladylike. She also said I was crazy even to think of going into the water; it was way too late in the season and I'd turn into an icicle in a moment. I didn't care. This was my first trip to the ocean, and I'd promised myself I would go in swimming.

We had lived in Harlem since June. Mama had decided that Philadelphia would be too painful, what with all her memories of Daddy and how he got killed, so we went to New York instead. Mama had asked Granma to come with us, but Granma didn't want to move. She was glad for us to be able to go, but Summit was her home, and a big change would be too much for her. Miss Alma helped her write us a letter every week.

In Harlem, you could walk down the streets and think you were in a completely different country from Summit. Black faces were everywhere, and people had nice clothes, money in their pockets, and smiles on their faces. Mama got a job at a restaurant, and we found an apartment in a building owned by a friendly lady from Savannah who said she was glad to rent to "home folks."

We had made a good choice, Mama said. The time was right, and we were free.

I missed Poppy. She had carried on terribly when we left, and as much as I wanted to go, that made it difficult. I understood just what Poppy was feeling, having a good friend move away. I told her to study hard so she could read and write well enough for us to write to each other. Poppy promised, and I did get three short letters from her, printed in awkward capitals. At the bottom of each one was a friendly note from Miss Johnson, who had helped Poppy write them. I wrote back, but after my third letter, I didn't hear from Poppy again.

I still missed Bailey. For a long time, I dreamed about him almost every night. When Mama told me we were moving, I was glad for lots of reasons, but especially because I thought that going to a new place would take my mind off of him. He had sent us two letters, which other people wrote for him. One was postmarked Savannah and the other Albany, Georgia. He said that he was all right. He had gone back to west Georgia to see if some of his brothers and sisters were still alive. He said he had found his brother Josiah and was going to stay with him and his family for a while before he started searching again.

"Coney Island!" shouted the conductor as the train lurched to a stop. Mama and I got off and followed the other train passengers. Right away we could see the Cyclone, Coney Island's giant roller coaster. Then we were at the boardwalk, lined with bathhouses, restaurants, food booths, shooting galleries, sideshows, and shops. Most of them were closed, but people strolled along, looking into windows and stopping to buy refreshments. I wasn't interested in those things because beyond the boardwalk was the beach, and I could see the ocean, sparkling in the sunshine.

"Come on," I told Mama, crossing the boardwalk and stepping down onto the sand. Then I was running toward the water. There was the gray-green sea, so much bigger than I had ever imagined, bigger even than Bailey had been able to describe. I half expected to see the majestic combers Mr. Armstrong had written about, but the waves were small, gently lapping against the light brown sand. I took a deep breath. Bailey was right about the salt smell. It was different from anything I'd ever known. I felt like laughing, running, and spinning around like a top, all at once.

I unbuttoned my sweater and sat down on the sand to take off my shoes and stockings. I jumped up, unfastened my dress, and pulled it over my head. I wished I could take off the uncomfortable swimsuit and go in the water undressed, the way Bailey had on that day so long ago down in Georgia. But other people were walking along the beach, and Mama would never have allowed it. The sand was cool on my feet. It scrunched when I wiggled my toes.

"So you're really going to do it?" Mama asked. She walked to where the water met the land. Bending down, she let a wave wash over her hand. She pulled back and gasped. "It's freezing! You'll catch your death of cold."

I walked right into the shallows. Mama was right— the water was icy.

I didn't care.

"One, two, three," I said to myself. Then I ran forward and plunged in. Underwater, I stuck out my tongue and tasted to see how salty the sea actually was. I opened my eyes and peered into the pale green glow of sunlight shining down into the water.

When I came up, giddy and gaping for air, there was Mama, standing just beyond the reach of the waves, watching me. "You frozen solid?" she called.

"Not yet," I called back. "I can still move a little!"

Mama laughed. "I don't know how you're doing it," she said. "But it's your day. Keep on as long as you want."

The ocean breeze on my wet skin was making me shiver. I dropped back into the water, but that was no better. I stood up quickly and started for the shore.

"Come on," Mama said. "Let's get you warmed up."

I ran to her. She wrapped me up and held me close. I looked at her, and I could tell she was proud.

"How was it?" she asked.

"Wonderful."

"You got your wish."

We stood together on the beach, gazing out across the water. I was wet and shaking, and the salt water made my skin itch worse than the bathing suit did.

None of that mattered.

The ocean, the world, and the future were mine.

About the Author

David L. Dudley spent ten years as a parish pastor in the Lutheran Church before turning to university teaching. He is currently a professor of African American Literature at Georgia Southern University. He has also taught prison extension courses. His published work includes numerous articles and essays; *The Bicycle Man* is his first novel. An avid gardener, cook, accompanist, and opera fan, Dr. Dudley lives in Twin City, Georgia, with his wife and their two younger children, whom they home-school.